MIDNIGHT SPRINGS

The Springs—Five

ELENA AITKEN

Midnight Springs

Also by Elena Aitken

Halfway Series

Halfway to Nowhere

Halfway in Between

Halfway to Christmas

Chapter One

IT HAD ONLY BEEN a little more than an hour since Bria
Sheridan had been accompanied up to what was a very fancy
room at the Springs hotel. The management said they would
comp the room, and so they should for all the money they were
swindling out of her grandmother, Mona. A flash of guilt
flared through her when she replayed the scene she'd caused in
the lobby. She hadn't really planned to let things get so out of
hand when she'd arrived at the resort and they wouldn't tell
her where her grandmother was. But she also hadn't planned
to go and personally haul her grandmother out of there. At
least not until the night before, when Mona told her over the
phone that she'd be staying at least for the next two months.
No way was Bria going to stand for that. Besides, until her
latest photo assignment was finished and accepted, she didn't
really have anywhere else to go. It seemed like a good solution.

The Springs billed themselves as a place with magic
healing waters, but all Bria could see was an overpriced spa
that prayed on the elderly who only wanted a miracle they
couldn't have—no matter how much money they spent. At

least she'd gotten there when she had; who knows how much money she'd saved her grandma from spending. But first she had to convince her tough-as-nails grandma of that.

There was a sharp knock at the door and Bria didn't even have to guess who it was. She doubted very much it was room service coming to bring her complimentary champagne and strawberries.

"Speak of the devil," she muttered as she opened the door. Her face transformed into what had to look like a very fake smile. "Grandma." She held her arms out to her favorite relative, but Mona only pushed past her into the room.

"Don't you Grandma me, young lady. Do you know what it's like to walk out of a therapeutic treatment where some handsome yet unseen young man with fingers like a god made me feel like a young woman again, only to be met by a security guard who tells you that your favorite granddaughter has just made a scene to end all scenes and has been escorted to a room where she's waiting to speak to me? Do you have any idea what that's like? Because it's kind of a buzzkill."

Instead of feeling chastised as she probably should have, Bria stuck her chin up and put her hands on her hips. "This is crazy, Grandma. This place is taking advantage of you."

"They're not and I can't believe they'd give you a room after the tantrum you likely had in the lobby. What they should have done was call Rhys Anderson and escort you to the Cedar Springs jailhouse."

Bria had to bite back a laugh at her grandmother's choice of words. "First of all, I don't think they call them jailhouses anymore. And second of all, you've clearly been here too long if you know the name of the local police officer. Or have you been the one who's had to visit the jailhouse recently?"

Bria hoped her lighter tone would defuse the tension. She hated there to be any bad feelings between them. Especially if she was going to convince her grandma to leave this place before it bankrupted her.

Just as she thought it would, Mona's shoulders relaxed and her face split into a smile. "Well, however you got here, you're here and I can't think of anyone I'd rather see. Besides, you come by that attitude naturally." Mona winked and held out her arms. "Come give your grandma a hug."

Bria let herself get pulled into her grandmother's embrace. It had always been her favorite place to be: her safe place, long after she should have been too old. She inhaled deeply; her childhood self hoped to get a lungful of her grandma's warm cinnamon fragrance that always reminded her of fresh baking. But it wasn't there. Instead, it was a pungent oil that filled her senses: a heady mixture of musk and flowers and something that was distinctly not her grandmother. Bria pulled away abruptly and tried to mask her shock.

"You're too thin." Mona pushed past her into Bria's posh room. She walked right past the pillow bed where Bria had dumped her small suitcase, and directly to a door she hadn't noticed before.

"Isn't Carmen clever?"

"Carmen?"

"The customer service manager, remember?" Mona rolled her eyes when Bria nodded. She'd met so many people since she'd stormed through the front doors of the Springs. They'd all been friendly, too. Starting with the very good-looking and slightly cocky—okay, really cocky—dirty blond, slightly scruffy in a way-too-handsome way guy. He'd thrown her off her game a little, which was probably a good thing considering she'd been behaving like a first-class brat. Even she could admit that. She blushed slightly with the memory.

"I remember. The pregnant one," Bria admitted. "Why is she so clever?"

Mona twisted the handle and pulled the door open to

reveal a room behind it. "She put us in adjoining rooms." Her grandmother lit up in a smile. "And wait until you see my suite."

"Suite?" Bria groaned at the thought of how much a suite would cost her grandmother in such a fancy place. She followed her through the door. "Do you really need a whole..." Her objections died on her lips as she took in the room.

Although Bria had been impressed with her own accommodations, her grandmother's suite was ten times bigger and fancier.

"It's pretty nice, right?"

Nice was an understatement, and by the look on her grandmother's face, she knew it too. Bria walked around the space. Her fingers trailed over the smooth polished wood of the dining table, the granite countertop of the kitchen and the... wait a minute. The kitchen?

"Why do you need a room with a kitchen in it?"

It was no secret that Mona didn't cook. Not even a little bit. It was a family joke that she could barely even heat up soup without burning it. The only time Mona ever set foot in a kitchen was for her once-a-year cinnamon bun extravaganza. It was a tradition ever since Bria was a little girl that her grandma would spend an entire day, from dawn until well into the night, mixing, rolling, rising, and icing cinnamon buns. They were always best fresh out of the oven and everyone who knew about it seemed to casually drop by that day to get a taste of her famous buns. But whatever wasn't eaten was frozen and brought out over the course of the year. Bria could never figure out why she insisted on only baking once a year when everyone so clearly loved her cinnamon buns, and she was so good at it, but her grandma insisted that by not doing it all the time, it remained special and people cared about it. There was some logic in that, Bria supposed, but as a little girl, all she could think of was the taste of the warm sticky bun in her mouth and the lingering scent that always seemed to cling to her grandma, even months after she'd cooked her last bun. The scent that was so obviously missing when Bria hugged her.

When was the last time her grandmother had baked? Was her arthritis really so bad?

Her grandma waved away the question. "This is how all the suites come. I usually take my meals in the restaurant. You should taste Jax's food. He is a miracle worker."

Jax. The name seemed vaguely familiar. But there was no way she would have met him. Nor did she want to. Bria had no intention to stay at the resort for one moment longer than necessary.

Not that there was anywhere else for her to go. The thought crossed her mind before she had a chance to block it.

"We'll have dinner down there and you can meet him. He's so funny and very talented in the kitchen, of course. Such a nice young man. Really, they are all so pleasant here at the Springs. I met the loveliest young guitar player. Simon Black but he called himself something else. I don't know why. The name Simon is perfectly good and—"

"Wait." Bria held up a hand to slow her grandma and her rambling trail of thoughts so she could catch up. "Black? You mean, Slade Black?"

There had been some sort of rumor about the famous guitar player who'd left his band and started up a solo career after falling in love with a single mom in a small town. "No way." All the pieces fell together. "That was here? And you met him?"

Her grandmother stood straight and patted her hair. "Not only did I meet him, but some would say I was instrumental in his life." She waggled her eyebrows and smirked.

Bria couldn't help it; she burst out laughing. "Of course you were, Grandma."

"You'll see. You stick around here long enough and I'll even help you, my dear."

The laughter died on Bria's lips. There was no help for her. She'd made sure of that. With her career on life support and her personal life little more than nonexistent, there wasn't much to help. But she wouldn't fail at everything. She took another look around the opulent surroundings; her gaze rested back on her grandma. No. She'd save her grandma from making the biggest mistake of her life and throwing her life savings down the drain. That she could do.

THE KITCHEN BUZZED with the usual dinner prep insanity. Something about a restaurant kitchen inspired chaos. No matter how much planning or preparation head chef Jax Carver had put into it, something inevitably went wrong.

"Chef. I can't find the mushrooms."

Jax looked up from the bowl where he'd been preparing a dry rub for the night's special. "What kind of mushrooms?" His latest hire, Doug, was a good kid, but some days Jax felt more like he was babysitting then preparing food.

"The white ones."

"Button mushrooms?"

Doug looked confused for a moment, and then nodded. "Yup. Those ones. I need them for the soup."

Jax forced himself to take a deep breath. "How many times have I told you, we don't—"

"I got this, Chef." Brent appeared out of nowhere and deftly slid between Jax and the prep cook. "Doug, we've been through this. There are five kinds of mushrooms in the soup, none of which are button mushrooms. Come on, I'll show you. Again."

Brent winked at Jax over his shoulder as he led the kid

away, and Jax made a mental note to buy his assistant head chef a drink later to thank him for doing such a good job.

The truth was, ever since Jax had gotten Stillwater up and running, he'd slowly started to pull back from the daily operations, allowing Brent more and more responsibility. Stillwater had been a hit, just like everything at the Springs resort had been. Sure, it had taken a lot of hard work and menu planning as he fine-tuned exactly what the upscale clientele would like to eat. But Jax had a knack for knowing exactly how to put dishes together. He was an expert at planning and creating a winning menu. But once he'd done that...where was the challenge?

Jax went back to his preparations with a sigh. That was the whole problem, the one that had eaten away at him for the last few months. He was getting bored again, which meant he'd want to move on to the next challenge, as was his pattern. No time to worry about that now, he thought as he added some cayenne to the bowl and mixed. For now, he'd focus on the dinner rush. He'd think about what he was going to do next later. Especially if his application at Angles, the latest hot spot in Los Angeles, was accepted. He mailed it off two weeks ago, which in of itself was strange, since he couldn't remember the last time anyone actually used the mail system. As well as being old school, the chef who ran the new venture was famous for leaving everything until the last minute, even so, Jax had hoped to hear by now.

"Hey. Is this a bad time?" The Harrison brothers Trent and Dylan walked through the gleaming stainless-steel kitchen toward him.

"Never a bad time for you two." Not for the owners of the Springs, Jax thought. But more than his bosses, they were good guys and the closest thing to real friends Jax had had in years. Moving around from restaurant to restaurant in as many cities didn't really allow for close friendships, which, for the most part, Jax was fine with. He'd never been one for guys nights and shooting the shit. Relationships of any kind were way more work than they were worth.

"What happened to you last night?" Trent lounged against the counter and grabbed a bun from the bread basket nearby. "I thought you were going to come back and join us after the baby shower thing. Not that it wasn't a lot of fun and all, Dyl." He shot his brother a glance and dodged the subsequent punch in the shoulder his brother delivered.

Jax had forgotten all about promising to meet up with the guys. He'd catered the baby shower for Dylan and his very pregnant girlfriend, Carmen, who happened to be the customer service manager at the Springs. After the party, he actually had agreed to go out and have a drink, which was unusual in itself, but what was even more unusual was being distracted by the very beautiful and extremely fired-up woman in the lobby when he'd gone to change. He grinned at the memory of the feisty brunette who'd been on a rant in the lobby the night before. He'd done his best to calm her down, but it was ultimately Carmen who'd shown up to smooth the waters. Jax had gone back to his apartment and forgotten all about drinks with the guys.

"I must have fallen asleep." It was a lie, but they didn't need to know that he'd been so distracted by a woman that he'd blown them off. "Sorry. Another time." Another lie. He'd already decided he shouldn't build their friendship any more than he already had. It would only make it harder to leave. And he was going to leave. He just needed to figure out when and where he'd go next.

Dylan nodded but eyed him suspiciously. "You alright?"

"Why wouldn't I be?"

Dylan was about to say something else, but Trent cut him off. "Of course he's alright. Don't be such a girl. Hanging out with your hormonal woman is making you sensitive."

Jax laughed but Dylan raised his eyebrows. "You'd say that to her face, would you?"

"You know I wouldn't."

They all laughed and Jax felt his mood lighten the way it always did around the Harrison brothers. The sound of a clanging pot brought him back to the present. He still had a dinner rush to prepare for. "What's up, guys? I know you didn't come here just to check on my feelings. Not that I don't appreciate it and all, but I do have to get back to work."

"True," Dylan said. "Your boss is a real dick."

Trent shoved him and stepped forward to hand Jax a piece of paper.

"What's this?"

"Augustus Bernstein," Trent said by way of explanation. And it was all the explanation he needed. Jax snatched the piece of paper and unfolded it, quickly scanning the text.

He had to read it twice before he looked up at Trent. "Augustus Bernstein? He's coming here?"

Trent nodded with a shit-eating grin on his face. "Pretty cool, right?"

"Don't let him take all the credit for it," Dylan jumped in. "I sent the request."

"Details, details." Trent waved his brother's protests away. "Either way, he's coming. Here. And you're going to impress him. Not only that, but with an Augustus Bernstein review, we'll be able to get some national and hopefully international media coverage for your amazing cuisine. Think of the boon for business."

Jax's mind spun. He'd always wanted to be reviewed by Augustus Bernstein. He was only the most notable food critic in North America. He was also notoriously selective about what restaurants he reviewed. And he was tough, too. But a review from Augustus would make his career. He could go anywhere. Cook anywhere. His career would be made.

And for a man who liked to be on the move...

"Wow," was all he could manage.

"Yeah, wow. More than wow. And he's coming next month, so you have a little bit of time to prepare."

"Next month?"

A month was not enough time. He'd have to plan a menu, test it and refine it. A month was not enough time for that.

"Well, three weeks, actually."

Jax looked up, mouth hanging open, and stared at Dylan, who'd just spoken.

"Three weeks?"

"It's all we could get and we were lucky to get that..."

Jax stopped listening as Dylan and Trent congratulated themselves on their achievement and what would ultimately be one of the biggest determining factors in Jax's career.

Now he just had to figure out how to make sure that was a positive thing.

CAUGHT up in the mania of the dinner rush, Jax didn't have much time to think about the letter and impending visit from Augustus Bernstein, which was a good thing because once he started to think about it, he didn't think he'd be able to stop. As it was, he was effectively able to push it from his mind and focus on pushing out perfectly plated and prepared meals.

On the last ticket, Jax wiped the rim of the plate, put it up in the window and breathed a sigh of relief. A few orders would trickle in for the rest of the night, but nothing his staff couldn't handle. He was just about to untie his apron strings when Sarah, one of the waitresses, appeared to pick up the food.

"Thanks, Jax. It looks great." She picked up the plates and as an afterthought, turned to him. "Oh, and there's someone at table six who wants to speak to the chef. She was very demand-ing." Sarah winked at him and Jax knew right away who it was.

Mona, the spunky guest they'd all come to think of as their resident grandmother, liked to personally thank Jax for every meal. She didn't always request to see him during the dinner rush, though. She was a smart woman, and knew enough to pull him away from the kitchen when it wasn't very busy and he could safely get away. Hell, even if he couldn't, he would for her. Something about the older woman made him happy. If only he could find that in a woman his own age...nah, who was he kidding? Even if by some miracle he found a woman who challenged him enough to keep him interested for more than one or two weeks, he'd never settle down. That would mean being tied to one place, and he'd seen firsthand with his own family growing up how damaging it could be to put all your eggs in one basket. He wouldn't make that mistake.

"Should I tell her you'll be out when you get a minute?" He'd forgotten Sarah was still there.

"No." He gestured to the steaming plates of food she held. "You take those out and I'll go say hi."

Sarah smiled and took off to deliver the food. Jax gave the counter a final wipe, left the kitchen in Brent's capable hands and took off his apron, throwing it into the laundry bin before he changed his mind last minute and circled back to the walk-in refrigerator. The pastry chef had worked on some new desserts, and he couldn't think of anyone better to spoil with a fresh piece of cheesecake. After he added a mint leaf and a raspberry for a garnish, Jax made his way out to the dining room with a smile.

Mona sat in her usual spot. It was crazy to think that a guest could have a usual spot, but she'd been at the Springs so long, she was starting to become a fixture. But what did it mean if he was getting attached to her? Just another reason he needed to leave soon. It was time to move on if he was getting attached. It always hurt less to take off sooner rather than later. And sometimes it did hurt. Leaving the Springs would be one of those times.

But he couldn't think about it yet. Especially not with the Augustus review looming. He'd sort it out. Later. First, Jax was determined to enjoy a bit of dessert with his favorite lady.

"I hear there was someone here who wanted to talk to the chef," Jax said as seriously as he could as he approached the table. "I hope there's not a problem with the—"

His words died on his lips as he noticed Mona was not alone. At first he hadn't noticed the striking brunette next to Mona, but he had seen her before: the night before in the lobby of the hotel, throwing what could only be equated to an adult tantrum.

"Oh. I'm sorry." Jax tried to keep his face as neutral as possible despite the fact that he desperately wanted to know why this beautiful and somewhat volatile woman sat with Mona. "I just assumed you were alone." He put the dessert in front of Mona and flashed an apologetic smile to the mysterious brunette, who watched him with a guarded look. It was an improvement: the last time he saw her, she'd been screaming at him. "I can get you a dessert, too, if you'd like?"

"Nonsense." Mona waved away his protests. "Jax, I want you to meet my granddaughter, Bria."

Granddaughter? The screaming tantrum started to make a little more sense in his mind as he remembered the way she'd been yelling about her...grandmother. Mona. It all made sense.

Well, not really. It actually didn't make any sense at all.

"It's nice to meet you." He held out his hand, choosing to assume she didn't remember him from the night before. Or at least, to give her a way out of what probably was an embarrassing situation for her.

"We've met." She raised one perfectly groomed eyebrow at

him but made no move to take his proffered hand. So, she was going to play it that way?

He couldn't help the smirk that pulled at his lips. He tucked his hand back in his pocket.

"How did you meet already?" A frown creased Mona's face. No doubt she'd been looking forward to making the introduction.

"I helped her—"

"He was—"

They spoke at the same time.

"After you."

Bria narrowed her dark eyes at him in a way that was probably supposed to come off as antagonistic, but Jax only found it incredibly sexy. Something about the woman, as angry and spirited as she clearly was, was also hot. Very hot.

She cleared her throat and pointedly looked away from Jax to focus on her grandmother. "I was just going to say that I met Jax last night when I arrived."

"Yes," Jax said as innocently as he could, enjoying the heat coming off the beautiful woman. "I'm just glad I was there to help out. Bria was very upset."

Mona's gaze flipped between them, a question in her eyes. Jax did his best to keep his face a careful mask of neutrality and as much as he wanted to, he didn't dare glance in Bria's direction. She didn't exactly seem like the kind of girl who'd appreciate being fooled with. But he couldn't help himself. It was too easy.

"Well, I do understand there was a bit of a fuss last night." Mona picked up a fork and slid it into the dessert. "I'm glad you were there for her, Jax."

He nodded solemnly.

"You know, Bria, Jax is very well thought of around here and it's always a good idea to have the best chef in town on your side." Mona winked at him and put the forkful in her mouth.

He couldn't help himself then, and he looked at Bria, whose pretty mouth, with her perfect lush lips, was turned down in a frown. He was pretty sure if her grandmother hadn't been next to her, she would have thrown her fork at his head, or something equally maiming. He winked at her at the exact moment that Mona let out a satisfied groan.

"This is so good, Jax." She shoved the plate toward her granddaughter. "You have to try this, Bria. Jax, you've really outdone yourself."

"I don't like dessert." Bria crossed her arms over her chest, which had the very fortunate side effect of pressing her breasts up to give Jax a generous view of her cleavage.

"Oh, I can't take any credit for the dessert. That's all Rose, my pastry chef."

"In that case," Bria smirked and she reached for the plate, "I think maybe I will give it a try."

He watched as she slid her fork into the creamy confection and put it in her mouth. His body reacted to the innocent action with a heat in his groin. He had no business having any kind of feeling for a woman who was so obviously angry about something, and clearly hated him on sight.

But there was no help for it; he was intrigued. Jax settled in and allowed himself to watch her reaction to the creamy deliciousness of the dessert. Bria had no idea the effect she had on him and she obviously had no idea that her face showed every little thing. Including how much she enjoyed her mouthful of sin.

Jax's mind flashed to a very different type of sin he could introduce that pretty mouth to, but Mona's presence snapped him back to reality.

"It's amazing, Jax. You tell Rose she has a winner." Mona

scooped up another bite before adding, "It's simply the most delicious thing I've ever tasted. Don't you think, Bria?"

Bria was quite obviously enjoying her own moment with the dessert. It was a rare thing when Jax saw someone enjoy food so thoroughly that they forgot where they were. It was incredible. And only served to make him want to get to know her even more. It took Bria a second to realize she was being spoken to but when she did, a blush crept over her cheeks.

"What?"

"I asked if you liked it." Mona's eyes danced with mischief. "But I think the better question would be if you wanted to be left alone with it."

Jax had to swallow a burst of laughter, and Bria's face burned brighter.

"Grandma!"

She shrugged and winked at Jax. "It was a fair question."

Bria's fork clattered to the plate and her face burned an even deeper red, but it was the flare in her blue eyes that intrigued Jax the most. He would have happily sat there all day, egging her on, but he had work to do—a lot of work, if he thought about the menu he'd need to prepare for the critic. Doing his best to suppress his smile, Jax pushed up from the table.

"It's been fun, ladies, but I should get going." His gaze locked on Bria, who'd managed to regain some of her composure. "I hope to see you again, Bria. How long will you be staying with us?"

"Not long." She straightened her shoulders and lifted her chin. Her long dark hair fell down her back. "I'll be taking my grandma and leaving just as soon as I—"

"Just hold on, young lady."

The two women glared at each other and it wasn't hard for Jax to see the family resemblance as far as the stubbornness was concerned. As much as he would have liked to stay and watch how the scene would play out, Jax was no fool when it came to women. Particularly angry women. He knew his cue to leave when he saw it.

He gave them each an easy smile and made his escape, but before he pushed the door back into the kitchen, he took one last look at the young woman who was now intensely arguing with her grandmother. Jax liked a challenge, and there was no doubt that's exactly what Bria would be.

Chapter Two

BRIA STILL COULDN'T UNDERSTAND how her grandmother had talked her into giving the Springs resort a chance, but arguing with the woman had never been a battle she could win. Which didn't stop her from trying, of course. She shook her head as she remembered the fight they'd had two nights earlier about making her grandma leave the resort. Her grandmother, of course, wanted her to give it a chance, and much to the surprise of both of them, Bria had relented.

Maybe it had been the lingering taste of the cheesecake on her tongue, but whatever it'd been, Bria'd agreed to give it a week. And when she'd said the words, and nodded in agreement, the look on her grandmother's face had been pure happiness. And isn't that why Bria had really agreed? She'd do anything for Mona. Even if it meant she had to pretend to be enjoying the overpriced, ridiculous resort with its calming, burbling water everywhere that was supposed to be soothing, but only served to annoy her.

Bria splashed her fingers in one of the offending fountains as she walked through the grand hallway toward the lobby. One entire wall was covered in glass and looked out toward the mountains, which she had to admit were stunning. The entire effect of the hall was actually incredible. Whoever had designed it knew exactly what they were doing. It was as if the outside was in. Or the inside was out. Either way, despite herself, every time Bria had walked through the hallway, she'd felt a little more relaxed. And that irritated her.

The lobby was quiet, with only a few people milling about, but when Bria walked toward the desk, she was greeted instantly by the very pregnant woman she'd met the first day. Carmen, her grandmother had said. It was her baby shower she'd interrupted with her tantrum.

"Ms. Sheridan, I hope you're enjoying your stay with us. What can I help you with?"

Bria looked at her feet briefly, ashamed of her behavior the first time they'd met. When she looked up, Carmen's eyes were bright and friendly, if not a little tired, and the smile of her face was genuine and helped to put Bria at ease. "I was actually wondering if there was a business center I could use? Or maybe some place in town I could have photos printed?" Her voice sounded clipped and bitchy, even to her own ears, but Carmen's smile didn't waver.

"We do have a small business center," she said. "But I don't think we have the proper facility to print pictures here at the resort." She tapped her finger against her lips for a moment. "But they have a one-hour photo printing service at the general store in town. Is that maybe what you're looking for?"

It was exactly what she was looking for. If her grandmother was going to make her hang out in the middle of the mountains for a week, Bria was going to have to work. She was already overdue with her assignment for her photo editor at *Lifestyle*, which wouldn't normally have been a problem, but given that she'd been late with the last three assignments, and her editor Kristie McNabb had hated all of her images, she was pretty sure if she didn't deliver on this latest project, she'd be looking for a new job.

"That's perfect."

Carmen scribbled down the name of the store and gave Bria some basic directions. "There's a shuttle that goes down into town a few times a day. Here's a schedule." She handed Bria a piece of paper. "Is there anything else I can do for you today?"

Bria was about to say no and turn away, but her conscience stopped her. She swallowed hard. "I just wanted to apologize," she said quickly. "I didn't mean to interrupt your baby shower the other night and—"

"Don't give it another thought." Carmen waved away her apology. "I understand you were upset and when our loved ones are involved, that's perfectly understandable."

Bria was pretty sure it wasn't understandable, but she wasn't going to argue with the woman. Particularly considering she'd caused her enough stress. "I appreciate you being so understanding," she said. "And I do plan on getting my grand-mother out of here as soon as possible, but my outburst wasn't necessary. I'm not sure what got into me."

Carmen simply smiled in response, so Bria kept talking. "When are you due?"

"Not soon enough." Carmen's hand went to her burgeoning belly and rubbed gently over the stretched fabric of her shirt. "But with any luck, it should only be another week or so."

Bria nodded in sympathetic understanding, although she had no idea what it would be like, nor did she have any desire to know what it would be like to have her body stretched that large. With another smile that she hoped was a little more genuine, she excused herself to figure out how she would get down into the town and print off some photos.

She always traveled with her laptop, but Bria liked to see

how her prints looked once they were actually printed. It helped her avoid any surprises with quality issues once the shots got to her editor. Or at least, that's what she told everyone. The truth was, Bria was old-fashioned and she missed actually holding a photograph in her hand. With all the computers and photo editing software, that didn't happen very much anymore.

Not that it seemed to matter, Bria thought as she found a padded bench to sink into while she studied the shuttle bus schedule. If she didn't come up with a really unique idea for a photo editorial, she was probably going to lose her position at the magazine. *Lifestyle* was one of the last print magazines left that actually employed staff photographers. But Kristie had made it more than clear that Bria would not be one of them for much longer if she didn't deliver and soon. The problem was, Bria had nothing except a few shots of some unique front porches she'd found. It was lame. It was boring, and it was anything but the cutting-edge story Kristie, and *Lifestyle* was looking for.

"Hey there."

Bria looked up from the paper she'd not even been looking at and straight into the dangerously good-looking eyes of Jax Carver. With such a big place, she would have expected that she could have avoided him. Was there any reason that she kept running into him? Only except the universe seemed determined to torture her, because she couldn't deny the way her body reacted to him and that smoldering way he looked at her, as if he found her incredibly entertaining. Bria swallowed hard, determined not to let him see that he had any effect on her. That was the last thing she needed. Or was it? The thought came so quickly and was so unexpected that Bria almost burst out laughing with the idea.

Instead, she forced a look that she hoped came off as casual and indifferent. "Hi."

"Going to town?" He gestured toward the paper in her hand. "Don't wait for the bus. I'll take you down."

Her body betrayed her with a shiver that ran through her at the idea of being in the close quarters of a car with him. She shook her head. "I'm good. I'll wait for the bus." Bria didn't look at him, but instead focused on the schedule in her hand. The next bus wasn't going to come for another three hours. She suppressed a sigh, but just barely, and continued to stare at the paper. She focused intently at the words, willing the schedule to change.

"You're going to wait three hours?" There was laughter in his voice, and that only served to irritate her more. "I can have you there and back in less time than that. Seriously, I promise I won't bite."

Something about his choice of words made her body thrill again, and she hated herself for it. Jax was charming, more handsome than she cared to admit, and a man. There was no reason she shouldn't be attracted to him. Except there was every reason. Men like Jax were trouble. They were the type of man who thought they could weasel into your heart and your life with a smile, a wink, and a touch. She had no time for that. Never had. Everything had been about her career. All the sacrifices she had made: the late nights, early mornings, going to bed alone. It had all been worth it. Her career was thriving. Or, it was.

The stark reminder of her looming deadline brought Bria back to reality. If she didn't deliver, it would all be over. She needed to get these pictures, and sooner rather than later. With a sigh, she looked up to his grinning and ridiculously handsome face. "Okay."

"Don't sound so excited about it. I promise, it won't hurt a bit." He extended her a hand, which she ignored. He grinned as she came to stand next to him, as if he expected her to refuse his help.

Bria stood tall and stiffened her spine. "I'm sure it won't." Her voice sounded bitchier than she intended it to. She didn't mean to be so harsh; she just couldn't help it. "Ice Queen," Peter, her last boyfriend—if you could even call what they were doing dating—called her when he broke up with her. He said she was emotionless and cold. But it wasn't true. She wasn't, she just—

"Unless you want it to." Jax's smile was dangerous and it heated something deep inside her. No, she definitely wasn't cold.

Bria pushed past him, needing some space in order to collect her thoughts. His proximity made it difficult for her to think straight and it infuriated her. Men didn't have that effect on her. Ever. She started to walk toward the front door and the fresh spring air that would give her some relief.

"My car is this way."

She turned to see that annoyingly handsome smirk on his face as Jax pointed in the opposite direction.

HE DIDN'T KNOW what it was about her that intrigued him so much. Maybe it was the way she so obviously didn't like him, or didn't want to like him. He was pretty sure she liked him. At least a little. But whatever it was, Jax liked it. He didn't bother to hide his gaze as he took in her stiff posture and the way she held herself slightly to the edge of the truck seat as if she was ready to flee at a moment's notice. She was nervous, edgy, and a little uncomfortable. Was it him? He knew damn well it was, and despite himself, he liked the effect he had on her.

Jax forced his gaze back to the road, guided his truck out of the parking lot and started down the mountain. "I'm a good driver," he said. "You don't need to worry."

"I'm not."

"Really? Is that why you look so terrified?" His eyes flicked to her and he had to swallow his laughter when she obviously forced herself to release her grip on the door. Changing tacks, he asked, "Where in town would you like me to drop you?"

"The lady at the desk told me there was a store where I could have some pictures printed."

"That would be the general store."

"That's really what it's called?" She turned to look at him and for the first time, her eyes weren't clouded with anger or distrust or whatever else was always going on in her head. She smiled a little and Jax couldn't help but think of how cute she looked when she allowed herself to relax.

"It is. And you should do that more."

Instantly, her eyes darkened again and she looked away. "Do what?"

"Smile." He turned back to the road to focus on the twists and turns. Not that he needed to. He could make the drive with his eyes closed, he'd done it so often. But maybe if he gave her some space, she'd loosen up a bit. But Jax wasn't known for his patience, and when after a few minutes, Bria still hadn't said anything, or even looked over at him again, he couldn't help himself.

"So what's your deal?"

"Pardon me?" He glanced over just in time to see her glaring at him. It wasn't much, but it was something and for whatever reason, even her narrowed eyes when she was angry with him turned him on. Clearly, he was a sucker for punishment.

"Seriously. You're in one of the most beautiful places on earth and from the moment you arrived, you've been pissed off. And frankly, I'd like to know why. So, what's your deal? What reason could you possibly have for being so angry?"

True, he didn't know her, and he definitely didn't know her story. But what he did know was that she was young, beautiful, and obviously had a grandmother who thought the world of her. She was staying at a world-class resort with one of the best spas at her disposal, and the woman could barely crack a smile. And for whatever reason, Jax needed to know why.

Bria made a snorting sound that could only be described as cute because he was positive it was intended to be anything but, and spun in her seat so she faced out the window. "I'm not pissed off."

He couldn't respond to that. Not without laughing, which he was pretty sure wouldn't be received well. But Bria must have realized how ridiculous her statement was, because after a moment, Jax heard a sigh, and her hand came up to her mouth as she tried to hide a smile.

"Okay," she said after a moment. "Maybe I'm a little pissed off."

Jax pulled to a stop, obeying the traffic sign, and used the opportunity to sneak a glance at her again. The frown was gone; the beautiful smile that seemed to light up her face was back. "Are you going to tell me why?"

To his surprise, she didn't immediately close up the way he assumed she would. Instead, she nodded. "My grandmother is the most important person in the world to me."

He nodded. It hadn't been hard to see how close they were, and Mona had spoken about Bria a number of times. It was obvious they were equally important to each other.

"And I don't like seeing her being taken advantage of."

Jax blinked hard. He wasn't sure what he expected her to say, but it hadn't been that. "What are you talking about? No one is taking advantage of Mona."

She tilted her head and her eyes narrowed. "Are you kidding me? She's been staying at that ridiculously expensive place for months with the promise that the water will cure her arthritis. Nothing is going to cure her arthritis. If the doctors can't do it, what makes anyone think that some hot water is going to make it all go away? She's an old woman. She's kind and sweet and just because she's desperate to feel better doesn't give anyone any right to fleece her of all her money."

"Whoa." Jax put the truck in park without bothering to pull over to the side of the road. Anybody who happened to be coming could go around him. "Nobody is fleecing anyone here. She's a grown woman who has chosen to stay at the Springs. That's her decision. Nobody is forcing her to stay. She can leave whenever she wants."

Fired up, Bria turned further in her seat and tucked one leg under her, so she faced Jax squarely. "She's staying because she's under the delusion that the spring water will heal her."

"Maybe it will."

"That's bullshit and you know it!"

"Healing takes place in a lot of different ways." He stared directly into her eyes, challenging her with his gaze. Jax wasn't talking about the physical healing of the spring water, which he had no doubt did hold some healing properties. But in his time in the mountains, and at the Springs resort, even he—a jaded traveler—had found that there was a whole lot more to this place then simple physical healing. A lot more. Even if most of the time he wouldn't admit it.

She looked as if she was going to argue again, and Jax found himself wishing she would. But instead she swallowed hard and turned out the window. "How far away is the store? I can probably find my own way back up to the Springs when I'm done."

"Nonsense. I'm not going to let you wait for the bus to come. I'll bring you back. The photos will take about an hour? I can meet you at the bakery whenever you're finished. I'm going to be just over an hour myself." It was a lie, and Jax couldn't be sure why he was lying to her, but suddenly he wanted to spend a lot more time with this woman. And if the

only way he could do that was in the cab of his truck, he'd
take it.

"You're sure? I don't want to keep you from all the important mixing and stirring and things you have to do."

Jax whipped his head around, ready to defend himself from
this woman, who not only questioned the legitimacy of the
Springs but now questioned his work as well, but Bria was smiling, a fun tease on her face. It took him a moment to realize
what it was but when he did, he raised his eyebrows and
grinned.

"Something like that." The truth was, she wasn't far off. He
was hoping to find Archer at the Grizzly Paw and talk about
some of his menu ideas for the upcoming tasting with Augustus. Specifically the ones that included wild game, because he
would definitely need Archer's help with that because he'd be
the one who would have to get it for him.

He pulled up in front of the general store and put the truck
in park.

"Cynthia will be able to take care of you. I don't think she
gets a lot of demand for printing lately. But if there's some kind
of line up, just tell her that it's a special favor to me. She's a
friend of mine."

"Oh really?"

It was obvious that Bria knew exactly what kind of friends
they were. Or had been. Once. Well, maybe twice. But regard-
less, it didn't matter. It wasn't going to be anything serious with
the tall redhead, no matter how sexy she could be on a Friday
night at the Grizzly Paw. As great as Cynthia was, she wasn't
his type. Specially because the only type Jax had was a temporary one.

"It's not what you think. Cynthia is a great girl, though.
She'll help you out." It was exactly what she thought. But he
really didn't want her to know that.

Bria looked at him again and searched his eyes for something before she grabbed her bag and opened the truck door. "Thanks. I'm sure I'll be fine."

She slammed the door behind her and Jax leaned over and quickly unrolled the window. "The bakery," he called after her. "In about an hour."

He laughed and shook his head when she just raised her arm in acknowledgment and kept walking.

JAX FOUND his buddy Archer Wolfe exactly where he knew he would—in the kitchen of the Grizzly Paw pub. The popular hangout was pretty empty this time of day, which was fine with him. He was happy not to make small talk with so many of the friends he'd come to make. They were great people, all of them. But the more Jax got to know them, the more he actually considered staying in Cedar Springs long-term. And he did not know how to do long-term. It wasn't an option.

"Hey buddy." Archer glanced over his shoulder when he heard the kitchen door swing open. "What brings you down the hill?"

Jax leaned up against a counter and crossed his arms. "I was looking for—"

"Let me guess." Archer held up a spoon from the pot he'd been stirring. "You were coming to steal my famous chili recipe, weren't you?"

Jax accepted the spoon from his friend because he'd be a fool to turn down Archer's chili. "You know it." He savored the small bite and mentally tried to figure out the spice profile that Archer used. No matter how much he'd tried, Jax could not figure out his secret. Which was probably okay, considering there wasn't much of a demand for chili up at the resort. He tossed the spoon into the nearby sink when he was finished with it. "One day I'm going to figure that out, you know?"

"It won't be anytime soon, my friend." Archer laughed. "Seriously, what brings you down? You have time for a beer?"

"Maybe a quick one. I need to be ready to go in about an hour." He didn't bother telling his friend why he was on such a time crunch because Archer would never believe that he had a date with a beautiful woman who just happened to be a guest at the resort. Jax didn't date guests. Not that meeting Bria to take her back up to the Springs was a date. Far from it, really, but he couldn't help but wish it was, which was a very unusual feeling for him. He couldn't remember the last time he'd been interested enough in a woman to actually want to sit down and talk with her. Jax was more a one night, have a few drinks, and have a little fun, kind of guy. And with Bria, he definitely wanted to do all of that, too. But he also wanted to talk to her and get to know her. He wanted that a lot.

He shook his head in an effort to clear it before Archer noticed something was up. "I have some menu planning to do." He changed the subject. "In fact, that's what I need to talk to you about. You'll never guess who Trent and Dylan lined up for the Stillwater?"

For the next forty-five minutes, the guys chatted over a beer and a bowl of chili, and before he left, Jax had cemented Archer's promise to get him some fresh venison for his special menu. Archer was the resident mountain man of Cedar Springs and the most talented hunter around. If he said he would deliver, he would.

Jax was just about to leave and head over to the bakery when Samantha Burke, the owner of the Grizzly Paw and Trent's girlfriend, wandered up. "Hey, Jax. Nice to see you." He stood and gave her a quick hug. "It's been too long since you've come and hung out with us on Sunday afternoon. When are you going to make it down here to hang out with us?" The group of friends was known for spending Sunday afternoons at the Paw catching up on each other's lives. It was their way of staying close despite their chaotic lives. It was all a little too close for Jax, who'd never had a group of friends like the ones in Cedar Springs. They were all nice enough, and if he did plan to make a life in one place, they would definitely be the people he'd choose. But he wasn't, so it didn't matter.

"I'll do my best to get down here soon." It was a lie and by the way Sam looked at him, she knew it too.

"I will hold you to that one day." She gave him a light smack on the arm. "Hey, Trent told me that Mona Sheridan's granddaughter was staying at the resort." In the few months that Mona had been in residence at the Springs, her gregarious nature had made quite an impact on the staff and even many of the people in town.

"Yup." Jax nodded. He was not about to get into a conversation with anyone about Bria. No way. He'd like to keep her all to himself. "Well, I should get going. I need to stop at the bakery."

"Isn't that a coincidence." Sam's voice lifted an octave. "I just came from there and I can't be sure, but there was a certain very pretty dark-haired woman who looked an awful lot like she might be related to—"

"Interesting." Jax gathered his papers where he'd been making notes on his menu. "That's quite a coincidence."

"Isn't it?"

He made his escape to the door but not before he heard Sam's friendly laughter behind him.

Chapter Three

FROM THE LITTLE Bria could tell, Cedar Springs was one of those towns she'd always hated. The super cutsie, everyone knows your name, and is right up in your business kind of town. Everything about it screamed sickly sweet, community love. Some people liked that kind of thing, but not her, no thanks. Bria liked her cities. The bigger, colder, and more sterile, the better. She didn't want anyone knowing what she was up to. What kind of misery would that be? Bria didn't even want to think about it. She'd done her best to create an environment for herself where she didn't have to worry about what other people thought of her. Besides her family. But even then, the only person's opinion who really mattered was her grandmother's. Her parents had always treated her more like an inconvenience, one they'd only barely tolerated until she was old enough to move out, which she did as soon as possible. She'd had a handful of friends in college, but it was easier to keep people at a distance, that way they didn't hurt you when you finally came to depend on them. Which they inevitably did.

The people who lived in Cedar Springs were probably

deeply unhappy and resentful of one another all the time. How could they not be when they were so obviously enmeshed in one another's lives so deeply? And really, if they knew everything about one another, that would only breed hostility.

Except it didn't seem to. In fact, the people Bria had run into, including Cynthia, who ran the store and turned a very bright shade of red when Bria mentioned Jax's name, seemed happy. They all smiled at one another and waved to people they ran into and even more interesting, they all wanted to stop and chat. No one seemed to be deeply protective of their personal lives. In fact, it was quite the opposite. They all wanted to share the details of their comings and goings with practically anyone they ran into.

More than that, they seemed to be personally affronted if you didn't feel quite as inclined to share. Like the woman who handed her the coffee at the bakery. Bria didn't remember her name, even though she was sure she'd been told what it was. The woman's kind disposition appeared to be a ploy to get Bria to share her own information, but she wouldn't be fooled so easily. She was a private person; she didn't need or want any friends in this backwater town.

Except for maybe Jax.

The thought flashed into her head before she could stop it and she almost burnt her tongue on her hot coffee. Where had that come from? She didn't consider Jax her friend. He was good-looking—more than good-looking, really. She wasn't naive enough to deny that, not even to herself. And sure, she might be a little attracted to him, but what woman in her right mind wouldn't be? But she certainly didn't consider him a friend.

Bria needed to focus. Until that moment, she hadn't even realized how rattled the town and the people had made her. But she didn't have time to be rattled, and she certainly didn't need the distraction. She put her coffee to the side where it would be out of the way and opened the packet of photos she'd just picked up from Cynthia. It hadn't been a problem getting the pictures printed quickly; in fact, the woman had seemed surprised with the request. It seemed even in a town as slow as Cedar Springs, people were still modern enough to go digital.

She knew it was a bitchy thought, and Bria pushed it out of her head, once again trying to clear her head as she laid the pictures out. Looking at the print photos was part of her process, and it used to be her favorite part. To see the images she'd seen through her lens translated onto the paper—there was something almost magical about it. At least there used to be. Lately, it didn't seem to matter what project she worked on: the magic was gone. And despite hoping for a different result with this batch, she knew even before the last photo was laid out.

Front doors.

Bria didn't even try to stifle her groan. There was no point. They were terrible. And anyone who happened to walk by would see that right away. What was she thinking with front porches? It wasn't trendy or riveting or particularly artsy, or really anything at all. She stopped short of throwing the pictures all over the bakery in her frustration. That wouldn't solve anything. She needed to hand in an assignment to Kristie. And she'd need it soon. She took another look at the photos. There had to be something she could use.

She tried to focus on the porches, but the longer she looked at them, the more ridiculous the entire project looked. The readers of *Lifestyle* weren't going to pay money to look at porches. Hell, she didn't even want to look at them for free, and she'd taken the pictures.

Her mind drifted to what she really wanted to do—and it definitely didn't involve porches. No. It involved Jax, and his strong arms and—

No.

She shook her head. She should be focused on her dying career, for goodness' sake. She couldn't go there. Not ever. It was ridiculous.

Was it?

Was it really ridiculous to allow herself to fantasize about Jax? It had been a long time since she'd been with a man. Way too long, really, and fantasizing about those big strong arms wrapped around her, his lips on hers, kissing her—

"Hey. Sorry I'm late."

Bria jerked up from the table so fast she almost knocked her coffee all over the pictures, which in hindsight might not have been a bad thing. She was positive her face was a violent shade of red. "You're not late." With any luck, he wouldn't notice her blush.

"Are you okay? You look a little—"

"I'm fine," she snapped. "I'm just trying to work." She turned her attention to the photos, picking them up randomly and changing the order, as if that would somehow make any difference.

Jax was quiet for a second and Bria could feel the heat of his gaze on her while he watched her.

"If you're going to be a minute, I'll grab a coffee."

Bria didn't look up, but nodded her agreement. The second she heard him walk away, she leaned back in her chair and let out the breath she'd been holding.

HER PICTURES WERE GOOD. But they were boring. Why anyone would want to look at a bunch of pictures of front doors was beyond him, but Jax could tell she had talent as a photographer. Not that he was any expert or anything, but even though the subject matter of the photos was dull, her composition wasn't. A house cat took center stage in one shot, a piece of mail in another. Ordinary things that made Bria's photos almost artistic in nature.

Not that he cared. Because he didn't.

"I'll take a black coffee, Suzy."

The baker, and owner of Dream Puffs, nodded at him and poured him a fresh cup. "What about a muffin this afternoon, Jax?"

He grinned and took the cup from her before he patted his stomach with his free hand. "Not today. I'm watching my girlish figure."

She laughed. "You're too thin for a chef, Jax. You need to eat more." They both knew she was kidding. Jax ate all the time, tasting his dishes, adjusting the flavors and making sure they were perfect. His love for food was why he spent so much time in the gym at the Springs and trail running the mountain paths. It was no mistake that Jax was in excellent shape. "You know what they say about skinny chefs?"

"Well, it's a good thing I'm not skinny then." Jax laughed along with her. "But how about one of those cinnamon buns? I don't think one of those will hurt." He winked and Suzy giggled before she got him his pastry.

Jax took his snack and sat down at Bria's table, moving his cup to the far corner, so it wouldn't get in her way.

"Do all the women in this town do that?"

"Do what?" He stuffed a piece of cinnamon bun in his mouth and held out the plate to her.

Bria shook her head. "Turn into little schoolgirls around you, or at the mention of your name?"

"Do they?"

She cocked her head in a way that he was pretty sure wasn't supposed to be cute, but really was. "You know they do."

Jax shrugged and took a sip of coffee. It was true that some of the women in Cedar Springs thought he was attractive, and sure, it was true that he might use that to his advantage sometimes. But with the exception of Cynthia at the general store, he'd never acted on his flirtation. And as far as Cynthia was concerned, she knew they'd never turn into anything more. That was part of what he liked so much about her: she wasn't interested in a relationship either. Even so, it had been months since they'd hooked up last. "What are you working on?"

"It's nothing." She rushed to slide the pictures together, piling them so Jax couldn't see them and even though the pictures themselves had been uninspiring, he couldn't help but wish she'd leave them. He wanted to see them. Because there was something about them. Or maybe it was the reaction she had to them.

"No." He grabbed her wrist and stilled it. He tried to ignore the heat in her skin, and the spark that shot through him just by touching her. "Leave them. Let me look."

"They're terrible." But she didn't pull her hand away. Instead, she slowly looked up at him. "They're really bad. I don't think you need to see them to know that."

Jax met her eyes and held them. He had no idea what he was doing. He knew the pictures were bad, if only because the subject was bad. And looking in her eyes, he could see the hope and expectation she tried so hard to hide, as well as something else—desperation, maybe—and now, knowing all that, Jax would have to lie.

To his surprise, Bria pulled her hand away and revealed the pile of pictures. Reluctantly, he removed his hand from her wrist, and picked them up.

He took his time flipping through them and picked out the ones that had caught his eyes originally: the shot with the cat and the lone piece of mail. Bria wasn't looking at him, so he took another pass at the photos, trying to see what she might have seen in them when she took the shots.

"They're bad, I know. You don't have to pretend they aren't. My editor will tell me soon enough anyway." Jax paused, and looked over at her. She still didn't look at him, but had her attention on her fingernails that she picked at with dogged determination. He waited, letting her continue. "She'll see them and I'll be without a job and then—I don't know why I'm telling you all this. You couldn't possibly care and—"

"What if I do?" And he did. He couldn't even explain it, but for whatever reason, he did care about this woman who'd been nothing but prickly with him from the moment he'd laid eyes on her. And he did like to lay eyes on her. And that was it, wasn't it? He liked a challenge, and Bria was definitely a challenge. But at that moment, it wasn't him that she needed; it was what he could tell her.

"They're good," he said after a second. "I'm not an expert by any means, but I know a good picture when I see it, and I like what I see. "

"You're full of shit. They're terrible."

Jax put the pictures down and looked up. "You want me to be honest?"

"Always."

Always.

For a moment, his mind drifted to all the ways he could be honest with her and his physical attraction to her, but she waited for his answer, so he focused and gave it to her. "You're obviously a talented photographer. I can see that in these two images particularly. It's not you; it's your subject matter. And I don't know what type of editor you're trying to impress or what your job is that you're going to lose, but..."

He drifted off, suddenly aware of how little he knew about her, but how much he wanted to know.

"I'm a staff photographer for *Lifestyle*. I'm supposed to deliver a photo editorial. The problem is..."

"These pictures."

"Yes." She laughed, but there was no humor behind it. "That's exactly the problem. And it's quite a problem."

"So why not take different pictures? When's your deadline?"

"I have a few weeks."

"A few weeks? You have lots of time and if you haven't noticed, you're in the most beautiful town in the Rockies and happen to be staying at the hottest and most exclusive resort around."

"And?"

"And, you have a camera, I assume."

"I do."

He could see the moment it finally registered with her, because her nose scrunched up in a way that was extremely cute and she shook her head violently. "I don't think so."

"Why not? You don't think it will be a good shoot?"

She didn't answer him, and he knew it was because she knew he was right.

"I hate the Springs."

That's right; she blamed the resort for her grandmother's happiness, which was beyond ridiculous.

"Didn't you promise Mona you were going to give it a chance? If I remember correctly, you agreed to stay with her for a week, so why not extend your stay a little bit and use that time to your advantage? I'll help you."

"You?"

"I know the Springs pretty well and I can show you around and make sure your talent is used for good." He'd had no intention of offering his services to her but now that he had, he couldn't think of any way he'd rather spend his time.

WHAT WAS HE THINKING? That was the question. And a damned good one too. After he dropped Bria off at the front reception desk, with a promise to meet with her the next day for the start of his tour of the Springs, he'd gone straight to the one place where he could think. The kitchen. His kitchen. Well, not his kitchen. But with the setup the way he wanted it, the free rein with the menu and state-of-the-art equipment, it was as close to his kitchen as any had ever felt. And Lord knew he'd been in his fair share of kitchens over the years. Jax grabbed his knives and a cutting board, and started to chop. It was his form of therapy. The more he thought, the quicker he chopped, until the knife seemed to fly over the board, and the veggies piled up.

Jax didn't have a plan for what he was going to cook; he didn't need one. It would come to him as he went and it didn't even matter; as long as he was cooking, he was thinking. And he needed to think. About what he was going to cook for Augustus, definitely. But mostly, what he was going to do with Bria.

Because despite the fact that she'd been nothing but prickly to him, he liked her. More than that, he was intrigued by her. And what her story was. But mostly, if he was honest with himself, he couldn't stop thinking about what those lips would taste like on his. And how her body would react under his hands as he—

"What smells so good in here? Don't tell me it's the special, because damn, that would be some special, and I'm hungry."

Jax didn't even have to turn around to know Slade was behind him. He'd become fast friends with the musician when he spent some time at the hotel early in the winter, but with his new touring schedule, it was hard enough for him to spend time with his girlfriend, Beth, let alone anyone else.

"Hey, man." Jax put his knife down, wiped his hands and pulled his friend into a quick man-hug back slap. "Not the special, but some soup." He waved toward the stove where his sous chef had already prepped the soup. "When did you get back?"

"Man, it's been a trip. After we left here, we were off to Vancouver, and then Seattle, and...we just got in last night. It was only a few days, but it's been crazy." Slade laughed, and while his schedule would have stressed Jax, Slade seemed to handle it fine. "Jules has some time off school coming up," Slade continued. "So she'll be coming with us to LA while I record some new singles." Jules was Beth's daughter, and Slade had taken to being a step-dad, or whatever the role was, a whole lot easier than anyone thought he would have. In fact, it actually suited him to tone down the bad-boy rock star image.

"Sounds good." Jax shook his head. "In a crazy kind of way. But I know you love it and I can't wait to hear your new stuff."

He turned back to his prep board and grabbed a sauté pan from the rack over his head, still not entirely sure what he was going to cook.

"Awesome. But that's not why I'm here."

Jax looked over his shoulder. "What's up? You just trying to scam some lunch?"

"Well, obviously. But mostly I need a favor."

"Favor?" He threw the onions into the pan with a pat of butter and some garlic. The sizzle and instant aroma hit him and just the way it always did, the scent calmed him and helped him relax. Now if he only had a chance to think things through. But first he needed to figure out what was up with Slade. "What kind of favor?"

"I need a very special dinner. And I mean, special. Not just *the* special, but an amazing, life-changing meal."

Jax opened the cooler and grabbed a pork chop. He set it to sear in the pan. "So, let me get this straight." He grinned. "You need something special?" Jax expected Slade to make a smart-assed comment in return, and when he didn't, he looked over at his friend, who wasn't smiling at all. He was totally serious. "Okay." Jax grabbed the tongs, and flipped the chop before he focused on Slade. "I can do special. What's up? Why so serious?"

"I'm going to ask Beth to marry me."

"What?" Jax fumbled the tongs, almost dropped them before he caught them just in time. "You're going to what?"

The seriousness gone, Slade's face split into a huge smile. "I'm going to do it, man. I'm going to ask her."

"Wow." It took Jax a second to process what his friend had said. Marriage? That was so...so...permanent. "You've only been dating for what, like a few months?"

"Three." Slade's smile only dimmed slightly. "But time doesn't matter when you find the right woman and damn—" He tossed his head back and looked up for a moment. When he met Jax's eyes again, there was no doubting the passion he saw in them. And if Jax, a man who'd never experienced that kind of love before, could see it, it was glaringly obvious to everyone else. "Beth is absolutely the right woman, man. I can't even begin to tell you the way she makes me feel."

Just listening to his buddy, a strange feeling washed through Jax, and he turned back to the stove. He felt sick to his stomach, as though he'd eaten something that had gone off. Not enough to make him sick, but enough to notice. But that wasn't the trouble. Jax sprinkled some seasoning on the pork. No. The way he was feeling had a lot more to do with Slade's announcement than anything else. If he didn't know better, he would think he might be jealous. But that would be ridiculous. Marriage was the last thing Jax wanted. After his parents' own marriage ended in a disaster that had almost ruined everyone around them, he'd vowed never to get himself in a situation where he could cause the same kind of wreckage. But Jax definitely felt something and it felt a whole lot like jealousy. Maybe it wouldn't be too bad to feel like that for someone? Jax turned away and shook off the feeling.

"I'm happy for you, man. For both of you," he lied. "Tell me how I can help."

WHAT THE HELL was she thinking? Bria was on her third circuit of the gardens and she still couldn't figure out what she'd been thinking when she'd agreed to Jax's crazy idea to photograph the Springs. Well, the idea wasn't crazy—even she had to admit the resort was amazing—but the idea of letting Jax show her around, that's what was crazy. How on earth could she work with him when she was so attracted to him?

There. She'd admitted it. Well, at least to herself, and wasn't that half the battle? It was true; she was not only attracted to the chef, she was ridiculous around him. She couldn't seem to formulate any reasonable thoughts in his presence, let alone verbalize them, which was exactly why she found herself in the predicament she was in. Her brain obviously couldn't work fast enough to come up with a solid reason why she shouldn't work with him on the photo project. And there were reasons. Good ones, too. But they would all sound crazy, even if she was able to say them out loud.

No.

Bria stopped at a wrought-iron bench nestled between two pine trees. The only reason she didn't want to work with Jax was because she was pretty sure she wouldn't be able to focus on her work with him so close. He was distracting. Everything about him was distracting. The way he walked with just enough swagger that you could tell how sure of himself he was, the sexy slow way he spoke to her as if every word held a deeper meaning, and the crazy way he looked at her, as if he could see past all the walls she'd so carefully put up and see the woman behind them. She'd never had a man look at her like that and damned if all those things didn't combine with a rock-hard body and a face so gorgeous that all together it created a force that made her insides twist in a way that she knew would be trouble.

She closed her eyes and dropped her head back. What would be the problem with getting into a little trouble? It had been a long time since she'd been with a man, and it's not as though she'd see him again after she left. It wouldn't really hurt anything. Bria sighed. Except she wasn't that type of girl. Never had been. *But what if I was? Just for a little bit?* The thought popped into her head so unexpectedly Bria almost laughed out loud.

What if?

Her phone ringing in her bag interrupted that train of thought before she had a real chance to explore it. It was probably for the best. Especially if Jax was going to help her. Her career had to be her focus. And speaking of career...Bria glanced at the caller ID. Kristie. She pasted a smile on her face and hoped it would come through in her voice.

"Kristie. Hi. I was just going to call you."

"Were you? With news of the amazing photo spread I'll have in my inbox by the end of the week, no doubt?"

Bria squeezed her eyes shut for a second. "About that, I wanted to—"

"No." Bria's stomach flipped and she waited for her editor to continue. "Bria, do not tell me right now that you don't have a great spread for me. Don't tell me that."

"Okay...I won't tell you that. But what I will tell you is that I have an exclusive line on a photo story that will blow you away and *Lifestyle* will—"

"So you don't have it yet?"

"Well, not—"

"Bria."

"Okay. No. I don't have it right now but I will. Soon."

Kristie didn't speak right away and Bria held her breath. They'd always had a friendly relationship. In fact, Kristie was the closest thing that Bria had to a real friend, but when it came to business, Bria wasn't naive enough to assume their friendship would triumph.

"What is it?" Kristie finally asked. "What is the photo story that will blow me away and make me change my entire editorial lineup for the next issue? Because you know as well as I do that if I don't have it on my desk by the end of the day, it won't be in next month's issue."

Bria nodded even though Kristie couldn't see her. "I know. But I promise, if you can give me the spot in the May issue instead, you won't regret it." God, she hoped she wasn't lying and Jax would help her come through with an amazing story. "I need a few weeks, Kristie, but it'll be worth it."

"What is it?"

Bria took a deep breath, exhaling slowly before she continued. "Have you heard of that exclusive new resort in the Canadian Rockies that claims to utilize the healing powers of the natural hot springs?"

"The one that's literally called the Springs? Of course I've heard of it. Slade Black left the Jacked Crackers after Christmas and hid out there. Everyone's heard of it."

"Well, what if I told you I could get a behind-the-scenes pictorial?" Bria wasn't sure exactly how behind the scenes she could get, but Kristie didn't need to know that right now. "I have a lead on an insider who can show me some of the secrets of the Springs and it would be exclusive." She also wasn't sure of that, but those were details she could work out later. First she needed her editor's approval.

"Wait. You mean, you can really get this story? Besides releasing some basic promo shots, the Springs hasn't let any media through their doors at all. What makes you think you can do it?"

Damn. She had no idea that the Springs had a media lockdown; Jax hadn't mentioned that. But maybe he didn't know when he'd promised to help her. Bria tried to sound as confident as she could, particularly because she suddenly wasn't quite so sure she could deliver. "Let's just say I know a guy."

Kristie laughed. "Whatever. Honestly, if you can get the story, I don't care how you do it. I'll be putting myself on the line for this, you know? So for both of our sakes, I hope your guy is good."

"Oh, he's good." Bria blushed, even though Kristie couldn't see her. "I mean...he'll be good." Ugh. That was worse. "That didn't come out right. What I really mean is—"

"He's got you a little off guard, does he?" Kristie laughed, and in that moment, her editor was gone and her friend appeared. "Well, good. It's about time a man had that effect on you."

"It's not like that."

"Well, if it's not, it should be. You know I love you, Bria, but sometimes I think you need to just stop thinking and take a chance. And I'm not just talking about your photography."

A million responses flew through Bria's head, but she kept her mouth shut. Because maybe Kristie was right: maybe she just needed to stop thinking so damn much.

Chapter Four

"GRANDMA? ARE YOU IN HERE?" Bria knocked as she entered the adjoining room. After a restless sleep, thinking about the magazine shoot, everything Kristie said, her dying career, and how all of it had been put squarely on the shoulders—the very strong, sexy shoulders—of Jax, Bria couldn't spend another moment alone. "I was going to get some breakfast. Are you hungry?"

No matter what she felt toward Jax, and how little it made sense, it didn't matter. She'd agreed to work with him and now she'd pretty much bet her entire career and her friend's on the photos turning out. So for better or worse, she was going to be in close contact with Jax, and maybe she'd surprise herself after all, and just stop thinking, the way Kristie suggested.

The thought made Bria laugh out loud. That was ridiculous. Everything Bria ever did was well-thought-out. It was how she'd gotten where she was. She wasn't about to stop now.

"What's so funny?"

Bria whipped around to find Mona coming out of her bedroom, looking as if she'd been up for hours.

"Just me," Bria said. "I was laughing at how ridiculous I've been about this whole thing." She waved her arms, taking in her grandmother's beautiful suite.

Mona lowered her eyelids and looked at Bria suspiciously. "I may be old, but I'm not stupid. What are you talking about?"

"Grandma." Bria laughed again. "I'm serious. I wasn't very understanding about why you're here and why you like it so much. But I promised you I would stay for a bit and make an effort and I will."

Her grandma smiled. "I'm glad to hear that. Even if I don't totally believe it."

"Grandma!"

It was Mona's turn to laugh. "Oh, Bria. You know I love you, dear. But I know you too well and I know that you do not change your mind about things so easily. So you might as well tell me what brought on the change of heart because you know I'll find out eventually."

Bria shook her head and dumped her bag on a nearby table. "I really want to make an effort for you. And I've decided to turn it into a bit of a working holiday, too."

"Ah, and there it is."

"No," Bria said quickly. "I didn't really plan it. But yesterday when Jax offered to—"

"Jax?" Her grandmother perked up and stared at her. "Now I think I understand."

"Oh no." Bria held her hands up and shook her head wildly. The last thing she needed was her grandma thinking there was anything going on between them. Especially considering the only thing going on was in Bria's head. There was nothing between them and definitely nothing for her grandma to *understand*. "It's not like that at all. He just offered to help me with a behind-the-scenes photo exclusive for the magazine. I need to turn in a quality assignment or—" She stopped herself. She really didn't need her grandma knowing her job might be in jeopardy. The woman had enough to worry about. No, some things she needed to just keep quiet about. "Well, I need a great assignment." Bria forced a lightness she didn't feel into her voice. "And Jax had the idea of photographing the Springs So, not only do I get to hang out with you, but I also get to take some great pictures."

"And spend time with a handsome man."

"Grandma."

Mona laughed and put her sweater on. Bria tried not to notice how she struggled with the buttons. The arthritis in her hands must be acting up. And wasn't the Springs' water supposed to be making it feel better? "What? I'm just pointing out the obvious," she said when she was done with her sweater "Now, why don't you come with me to breakfast and meet some friends of mine?"

Bria shrugged. "Sure. Who are we meeting?"

"They're a sweet couple. You'll like them. Beth's a sweet girl, about your age actually. She was my therapist when I first came to the Springs. And Simon is her boyfriend. I made him some mittens to keep his hands warm. He's a guitar player and it was very cold when he came here. Silly boy wasn't used to the mountain weather and it was almost impossible for him to write songs if his fingers were cold."

Bria froze, her hand on the doorknob. "Wait?" She remembered her grandma talking about Simon or more specifically, Slade. "You're talking about Slade Black, aren't you? The famous guitar player who left his band in the lurch and ran off?"

Mona waved her hand in the air, dismissing her. "Yes, yes. I told you that already, didn't I? Some call him Slade. But I refuse to. His name is Simon. Slade is such a silly name." She shook her head and Bria just shook her head in disbelief. "He's lovely and I want you to meet him. Come on."

It took Bria a moment to process that her grandma was

about to casually introduce her to a superstar celebrity. Her feisty grandma pushed past her and out in to the hall.

"Are you coming?"

Bria nodded and quickly followed her out. If nothing else, it was going to be an interesting few weeks with her grandma.

THE MAIN HALL was one of Jax's favorite parts of the resort. Its wall of glass showcased the mountains outside so clearly it felt as if they were inside, and you were walking right through them. In all the places he'd worked all over the world, he'd never seen anything quite as spectacular. As far as amazing settings to work in, the Springs took it, hands down. Which was just another reason why he was crazy to leave.

He cleared the thought before it could take hold in his head. No. He needed to leave. Too long in one place was never a good thing for him. Even if everything at the Springs felt right. The feeling would pass. It always did.

Jax slowed his pace and trailed his fingers in one of the many fountains scattered in the hall. The whole theme of peace, tranquility, and water ran throughout the resort and was one of the reasons everyone felt so relaxed there. Of course, the therapeutic water helped with that, too. It didn't matter what Bria said, or how skeptical she was: the water was healing. She'd come around. He knew it.

Just thinking of Bria put a smile on his face. There was something about that girl. She was so different from other women he'd been with. Mostly in the way that she was trying so hard to make it clear to him that she did not want to be with him. But unless his radar was totally off—and it rarely was— she did want to be with him. She was just fighting it. And that was okay with him because he looked forward to convincing her.

Despite taking his time as he walked through the hall, it wasn't long before Jax found himself outside the Stillwater restaurant, ready for a day creating dishes that would blow the minds of everyone who would taste them.

Ugh. He had to stop himself from groaning out loud. Normally he couldn't wait to get to work in the kitchen, but ever since Slade charged him with finding a perfect meal to propose to, his mind had totally gone blank. Never mind the whole thing with Augustus, and the review that would undoubtedly change his life. Whether it would be for the better or not was still up in the air.

Jax stared at the entrance to the beautiful world-class restaurant he'd been in charge of since it opened. He loved the Stillwater. The kitchen was perfectly designed and filled with top-of-the-line appliances, and the staff was amazing and talented in their own right. From the moment he'd set foot in that kitchen, he'd been creating amazing dishes. His creativity was at an all-time high ever since he'd been in the mountains.

Which was why it was extra annoying that he'd gone totally blank. He ran a hand through his hair, tousling it further, and took a deep breath. He was about to walk away completely and forget about trying to work, when a familiar dark head of hair caught his eye.

Bria.

A smile crossed his face and suddenly the idea of going up to his apartment, or anywhere else, was far less appealing. It hadn't even been twenty-four hours since he'd last seen her, but it didn't matter. Suddenly, that seemed like too long. He made his way quickly through the restaurant toward Bria and it was only when he was too close to turn back that he saw she wasn't alone.

"Good morning," he said, addressing the table.

"Hey, buddy."

Slade popped out of his chair and shook Jax's hand. "It's

good to see you." He winked dramatically and Jax had to swallow a chuckle. As if anyone would fall for Slade's terrible acting. It was a good thing his buddy was a musician, and not an actor.

"Hey, Slade. Beth." He bent and kissed Beth on the cheek. "Mona, Bria." His eyes lingered on Bria a moment too long. "It's nice to see you all again." He turned to Beth. "When did you get back?" He played along with Slade's charade. If he was planning a special proposal, Jax would not be the guy to ruin it.

He didn't sit, but moved around the table instead so he stood directly across from Bria. He offered both her and her grandmother a smile.

"Jax, it's been a total whirlwind," Beth said. "But I wouldn't trade it." She smiled up at Slade with so much love in her eyes, that if Jax wasn't a friend of theirs, he might have rolled his eyes a little. But it was nice to know that love did exist. Not that he needed it or wanted it. But for those who did, it was good to know it could happen.

He stood and made small talk with them for a few minutes before he allowed his eyes to lock on Bria again. "Are you ready to get started on that project we talked about?"

His question took her off guard, and for the first time since he'd arrived, she made eye contact with him.

Yes, she was definitely fighting something when it came to him.

"Now?"

He shrugged, trying to appear nonchalant. "It seems like a good time. If you're not too busy." He hadn't planned to get started with things so soon, and Lord knew he had a million things to do in the kitchen. None of that mattered. The second he saw her, he couldn't wait to be alone with her again. And there was no time like the present. The kitchen and his menu planning could wait. Jax purposely avoided Slade's eyes.

Bria stared at him; her dark eyes searched his for something. Finally, she nodded. "Why not? Grandma, are you going to be okay for a bit?"

Mona bristled, but followed it up with a grin. "Young lady, what makes you think that I wouldn't be okay without you? I've managed to get along just fine around here without you for the last little while. I think I'll find something to keep me occupied."

Bria smiled and shook her head. "That's not what I meant, Grandma. But I'm glad you'll be fine. I'll see you later, okay?"

"You'll see me for dinner," Mona stated. "And then I'm sure you'll tell me more about this little project of yours with Jax." The older woman eyed him suspiciously and he gave her a killer smile in return.

He moved back half a step while Bria pushed away from the table. She stood so close, he could smell the scent of her shampoo, and it took all the willpower he had not to pick up a handful of her shiny black tresses to let them slide through his fingers just so he could see whether they were as soft as they looked.

"Excuse me." He still didn't move back, so Bria had to turn to the side to shimmy past him. If she noticed, she didn't let on. "I'll just run up and get my camera," she said.

Jax held her eyes. "I'll meet you outside," he said. "By the garden doors."

Bria nodded and turned to leave after giving her goodbyes to everyone else at the table. He watched her go, and it wasn't until Slade cleared his throat that he turned around again.

"Sounds like you have an interesting day planned."

Jax looked around the table. His gaze flitted quickly over the questioning eyes of Mona. "I'm just helping her with something. It's not a big deal."

He was almost positive that nobody believed him. Hell, he wouldn't have believed himself. But he also didn't plan to stick around to get grilled about it. "I should go," he said. "Have a great day and don't forget to come back for lunch. The soup will be fantastic."

Jax was mid-step in his retreat when Slade called out behind him. "Jax, I'll catch you later to chat about that thing."

He didn't turn around, but offered a nod in acknowledgment. There was no doubt. He was going to have to think of something special for his friend. But it would have to wait until later. First, Jax planned to focus totally on a certain dark-haired woman.

Chapter Five

SHE'D COME to the garden from a side door, so Bria was able to walk up without being immediately detected. When she saw Jax on a bench, his back to her, she paused for a moment before she announced herself.

Pull it together, Bria. You've never gone all girly around a guy before and you're not going to start now.

She took a deep breath and pulled herself together. She didn't have the luxury to lose focus around Jax. There was way too much on the line. Bria exhaled, flipped her hair over her shoulder and walked toward him. "You surprised me today."

Jax popped his head up. It was his turn to be surprised. "Hey." He jumped to his feet. "I surprised you? How so?"

"I didn't think you really meant it when you offered to help me out."

He ran his hand through his hair, causing it to flop over one eyebrow, and her stomach did an annoying flip. *No.* She chastised herself. *Focus.*

"Of course I meant it. I never make offers I don't plan on following through with."

Was it just her or were his words loaded with a lot more?

He offered her a hand. "Shall we?"

Bria hesitated. She wanted nothing more than to put her hand in his and feel the heat from his skin seep into hers. But she also knew it would be nothing but trouble. If his touch affected her half as much as she thought it would, there would be no way she could concentrate on her assignment. And that's all that mattered.

She shoved her hand in her pocket and left his hanging. "Let's get going."

If he was put out, he didn't show it. If anything, his cocky smile told her he was enjoying the subtle torture he was playing out on her. He led the way, and Bria fell into step next to him. They walked side by side, so close that every nerve ending in her arm was aware of his proximity. Hell, they might as well have been holding hands. She might combust from the heat he put out. Or maybe that was the heat inside her? Either way, it wasn't going to happen.

Bria shifted to the side and hoped it wasn't too obvious.

"Are you okay?"

Apparently it was obvious.

She pasted a smile on her face, which would only make things stranger, because she was terrible at hiding her feelings on her face. "I'm fine. Where are we going?"

Jax eyed her suspiciously, the pull of a smile at the corner of his mouth. But he didn't push things, and for that Bria was thankful.

"I thought I'd start simple," he said, "and show you around the grounds. Spring is one of the best seasons in the mountains. It's right up there with summer, fall, and winter."

She whipped her head around to look at him, and he laughed.

"Seriously, every season in the mountains is awesome. But spring is one of my favorites. And I plan on showing you why."

She laughed along with him. He was just easy to be with.

Obviously passionate about the resort, it was easy to see the beauty in everything he pointed out. Bria pulled her camera out of her shoulder bag, adjusted the settings for the daylight and snapped pictures of everything Jax pointed out.

For the next hour, they walked slowly around the gardens, just starting to come to life after a long winter, and the wooded paths that led from the main building and afforded beautiful views of the valley and the surrounding mountains. She was so lost in taking pictures and listening to everything Jax told her, Bria didn't even notice how far or high they'd gone until they broke through a stand of trees and stood on a rock shelf that overlooked the valley and town below.

"Wow." She took another step toward the edge, but left herself enough ground to feel safe. "It's…just…wow."

"Pretty spectacular, right?" Jax came to stand just behind her and for the first time since they'd started out, Bria was once again acutely aware of his presence. And mostly, what it did to her.

She shivered despite the heat of the sun and the exertion of the hiking that had warmed her through. "It is." She raised her camera to her face and concentrated on capturing the view.

Jax waited her out and when she lowered the camera, he was still next to her. They stood in silence for a moment and took in the view.

Finally, his voice low and full of heat, he asked, "Is it helping?"

"What?"

"This. You and me."

His words caused her stomach to flip and a blush to creep down her neck. Of course he meant the photos, not them. Not that there was a *them*. She shook her head.

"It's not?"

"No," she said quickly. "I mean, yes. I didn't…never mind."

"Which is it?"

She turned to see him stare at her, his eyes locked on hers. With him blocking her retreat, there was nowhere to go.

He reached out and tucked a strand of hair behind her ear. His fingers lingered on her cheek for just a second. The move was so casual, it was as if he'd done it a million times before. But he hadn't. Her body would have remembered that reaction and it was all she could do to keep her knees from giving out. She bit her bottom lip in an effort to force her body to stop betraying her.

"Well?" he asked softly. "Is it helping?"

She swallowed hard and nodded. "The pictures will be beautiful. I'm excited to see how they turn out, and—"

Jax put his finger on her lips to quiet her. The move was so unexpected and so incredibly sexy, it took all her power to keep from moaning or making some other equally mortifying sound. It was simply not fair what this man did to her.

Jax slid his hand around the side of her head, to cup her cheek. His touch was tender, but he held her with authority. There was no doubt of that. "You know what I think?" His voice was gruff, and she felt the heat of his breath when he leaned in. "I think it's helping you more than you even know."

His lips were only a fraction of an inch away and everything in Bria longed to bridge that minute gap and connect with him. To hell with all the reasons she'd convinced herself to stay away. Or the fact that she'd only known him for a few days. She closed her eyes but the second Jax's lips brushed hers, she put her free hand up between them and pushed him back, clearing her way back to the safety of the trees.

She wouldn't kiss him. She couldn't, because if there was one thing Bria knew about herself it was that she'd never felt such a pull toward a man before and there was too much riding on her photos to let anyone get in her way. And there was no doubt that's exactly what Jax would do. Get in the way.

"Bria."

She wouldn't look at him. She'd fold if she did. Instead, she busied herself with the settings on her camera and kept her back to him.

"Look at me."

She shook her head. "I need to find the right aperture for this shot and if I don't get it just right, it won't turn out. With the wrong exposure, it will——"

Jax grabbed her by the arm and spun her around so quickly it took her brain a second to catch up. He had one arm wrapped around her back; his other hand cradled her face. His thumb stroked small circles on her cheek and when she opened her eyes, just as predicted, she was lost.

His lips crushed hers in a hot, hungry kiss she was all too eager to return. He threaded his fingers in her hair and held her to him as his lips explored her mouth, tasting and seeking. She responded greedily, tired of fighting whatever it was between them. And whatever it was between them, it was hot. Every nerve ending in her body was alive and each one had a direct line to her core.

He pulled away, gently sucking on her bottom lip as he did so but he didn't release the grip his arms had on her and as far as Bria was concerned, they could stay that way all day. The kiss had driven out any protests she may have had about why there couldn't be a *them*. In fact, it had driven out any and all thoughts that didn't involve another kiss.

KISSING BRIA HAD BEEN A RISK, but damn, it was worth it and by the satisfied look on her face, she thought so too.

"I've wanted to do that all afternoon."

"Only for the afternoon?" she teased, and the devilish smile she gave him caused a twitch in his groin. Kissing her seemed to bring out a whole different side of her. A side Jax was pretty sure he was going to like.

"Make no mistake," he pressed a soft kiss to her forehead, "I've wanted to do that from the moment I witnessed your tantrum in the foyer."

She stiffened. "It was not a—"

He silenced her with a much stronger kiss on her lips before he smiled. "It was," he said. "But I like that side of you."

Bria's lips twitched up in a wicked smile. "Do you?"

"I do. It's very hot." Jax let a hand slide down her back to cup her ass, which he gave a squeeze. "You're very—"

She slid out from his grasp, and he would have cursed the loss of her, but Jax knew what it was—a chase. And he was definitely up for it. He'd chase her; hell, after that kiss, he'd chase her all over the mountains if it meant feeling that heat again.

"Ready to go, then?" He smirked when she look surprised. No doubt she'd been expecting some sort of protest from him. But he wouldn't give it to her. Not yet. He knew how the game was played and what women wanted.

Although most women were not Bria.

"I think I got what I needed here." She licked her lips and Jax had to swallow his growl and need to pull her right back into his arms. Damn, the woman had no idea what she did to him.

"I bet you did." He took a step past her toward the trail before he turned and held his hand out to her. "Shall we?"

"Absolutely."

He wasn't surprised when she didn't take his hand but pushed past him to take the lead on the trail. But he'd be damned if he was going to let her go so easily. In one step, he reached forward and took her hand to jerk her to a stop. "One more thing," he said gruffly as he pulled her toward him. Her body pressed up against his and she didn't push away, but looked up at him with those deep eyes that gave away nothing.

"And what's that?"

Jax ran his hand down the side of her face and kissed her again. It was hot, insistent, and absolutely guaranteed to leave her wanting more. Which is exactly what he wanted when he reluctantly pulled away.

"Now I got what I wanted, too."

Chapter Six

IT HAD BEEN ALMOST a week since Bria and Jax had started to work on their project. Almost a week since they'd shared their first kiss and almost a week since Bria's mood had changed considerably. Because that first kiss hadn't been their last. Far from it. It had just been the beginning. Every day, they'd managed to sneak away for a short walk so Jax could point out some small feature of the resort that anyone could have seen on their own. But somehow when Jax pointed it out, it was different. As if she could see the simple fountains or the treatment pools through different eyes.

But maybe it wasn't the eyes at all, but the feel of his lips on hers when he kissed her, his arms holding her tight, and the way her body all but burst into flames when he touched her. Maybe those were the things that helped Bria to see the Springs in a much different light.

Whatever it was, she wasn't the only one who'd noticed.

"You seem happy." Mona lay on her floor, doing her stretching exercises with a large ball that the physiotherapists had provided for her. Bria watched as her grandmother rolled backwards, her head hanging upside down.

"I am." Bria flopped down on the couch. If anyone else in her family had uttered those words to her, she instantly would be on guard but she'd always been more connected to her grandma. She might tease her until she begged for mercy, but it was never malicious. Unlike other family members. "You were right. It's nice here."

Mona rolled back and forth on her spine, and her arms waved out to the side. When she finally stopped moving, she let out a sigh of pleasure and her eyes found Bria's, albeit upside down. "I told you so. But something tells me you're enjoying things here for a very different reason than I am." She grinned wickedly and rolled away before Bria could say anything.

She hadn't tried to hide her time with Jax, but she also hadn't made it a talking point between her and her grandmother either. There was a very fine line between telling Grandma about a work project with a man and telling her about the way that very same man held her close and whispered dirty things in her ear. Dirty things they'd yet to do together, but Bria's resistance wavered a little more every day. She could hardly remember why she'd protested things with Jax in the first place. Something about focusing…it didn't seem to matter anymore.

"What are you doing, Grandma?" Bria twisted her head around in an attempt to follow Mona's convoluted stretch. "It looks barbaric."

Mona groaned in obvious pleasure. "Oh, but it feels so good." She rolled the ball farther backwards. "Josh taught me how to stretch out my spine to relieve the pressure on my arms and legs. It helps with the pain and would you believe it's actually given me some mobility back?"

Bria shook her head. She wasn't sure she did believe it. As much as she was coming to enjoy the Springs and everything the resort had to offer, she was still unconvinced that there were any actual healing properties in the water the way they claimed. Sure, it was relaxing and beautiful and everything about the place was serene and offered a sense of therapy for your body and soul, but healing? She remained unconvinced and it still prickled at her that her grandmother spent so much money on a wild-goose chase.

"Are you still taking the meds the doctor prescribed?"

Mona gave her an unimpressed look, no doubt because Bria had once again dismissed the stretching. "No." She rolled herself forward so she was seated on the ball. "As a matter of fact, I haven't taken them all week."

Bria shot up to a sitting position as well. "What? Grandma. You have to take them. If you don't take your pills, the pain will get worse, and you might get to a point where you can't—"

"I know very well what could happen. But Bria Sheridan, young lady, if I've taught you anything, I would hope to God it's been that you can't live your life full of 'what-ifs'. Every day is a gift. Go out and live it and stop worrying so bloody much."

"I don't worry." Even as Bria spoke the words, she could taste the bitterness of the lie. She worried. All the time. Except in the last week. In fact, if she stopped to think about it, she hadn't given much thought to what-ifs or worry the way she normally did. At least not when Jax was around. Hell, she'd even stopped worrying about all the reasons she shouldn't be fooling around with him. And there were a lot of reasons. But then again, there were a lot of reasons that she—

"Bria." Her grandmother's voice brought her out of her brief daydream and she focused once again. "You're going to give yourself an ulcer or worse, if you don't relax a little. And really, what could be so stressful in your life? You have a fabulous job, doing what you love, a great family…well, your grandma's pretty damn great anyway. You're young and beautiful. What do you have to worry about?"

For a moment, Bria considered telling her grandma about her job and how the project she was supposed to be focusing on and devoting all her creative energy to was supposed to save her job, and the job of the only woman she called a friend. For the slightest of moments, she thought about unloading all of that, if only to show her grandma that she wasn't overreacting. She did actually have some stress and worry in her life. But she didn't.

She kept her mouth closed and simply shrugged.

"If I was your age, oh…the things I could do." Mona laughed at herself before she looked at Bria again. "Seriously. You're young, smart, gorgeous, and talented. Not that I advocate tying yourself down with a man—Lord knows they're more trouble than they're worth most days—but I have to say, it's beyond me why I've never met one of your boyfriends."

"Because I've never had one." Not one worth introducing you to, anyway, she almost added, but didn't.

"I find that hard to believe."

Bria shrugged again.

"Well, that Jax sure has his eye on you, and he's a real catch."

It was Bria's turn to burst out laughing. "He's a catch, Grandma? Really?"

"Well." She tilted up her chin in mock annoyance. "He can cook and in my books, any man who can cook is a real catch."

"I'll keep that in mind." Bria tossed her hair behind her shoulder and looked over at the clock over the mantel. "I should go soon."

"Hot date?" Mona stood up and started a series of stretches that included windmilling her arms out to the sides.

Bria shook her head, but the truth was she was going to meet Jax. He'd promised her an inside look at the kitchens and she planned to take some great shots of the masterpieces he was going to prepare for her. He'd said something about her helping him out with something, too. Whatever that meant.

"You're blushing."

"I am not!" Bria's hands flew to her face. Damn. She was flushed. She was blushing.

"You don't have to pretend on my account." Mona tilted from side to side. "I'd be blushing too if I was going on a date with Jax."

"It's not a date."

"Okay."

"Grandma."

Mona stood upright and stared at her granddaughter. "Would it be so bad if it was?" she asked. "I may be an old lady, but my thoughts aren't old, I can assure you. And you know I love you, Bria. But like I said earlier, you're far too young, successful, and beautiful to worry so much. If you like being with him, and he likes being with you, go with it. Dammed what anyone else thinks."

She was so serious, and so unlike her normal self, Bria stopped and let her grandmother's words sink in. After a moment, she nodded. "Okay."

"Okay?"

"Okay. I will. You're right."

"I am?" She looked momentarily stunned before she cleared her throat and straightened up. "I mean, of course I am." She crossed the room and sat next to Bria on the couch before she took her hand in her own. Bria could feel the gentle shake in her grandma's tentative grip, but she ignored it and focused on the older woman. "I know your parents were hard on you, Bria. Their heart was always in the right place, even if their techniques weren't. And they had no right to ever make you feel like you had to be someone you aren't, or sacrifice your own happiness for the pursuit of someone else's idea of success. They were wrong, sweetie."

Bria felt hot tears prick at the back of her eyes, but she blinked them back. She'd long since given up on crying over her parents. "Thank you, Grandma."

"I mean it, Bria. Don't give up on yourself. I know there's a girl in there who wants more."

This time the tears that threatened weren't because of her parents, but because her grandma had hit close to home. A little too close to home. She did want more. At least she thought she did. She just didn't know what that looked like yet.

THE LAST WEEK spent with Bria had been fun. No. It had been more than fun. It had been amazing. Jax couldn't remember the last time he'd enjoyed the company of a woman so much when they weren't even having sex.

Not that he didn't want to. God did he want to. Every fiber in his body twitched when he just held her hand, and kissing her was an exercise in restraint because once he got a taste of her, all he wanted to do was push her up against the nearest wall, taste every inch of her body and claim her for his own.

Damn. Just thinking about her made him lose focus and the last thing he needed to do was lose focus. More than he already had. Although the last week with Bria had been great in a lot of ways, it had definitely not been great for his productivity. He had two menus to plan and they both had to be spectacular. Better than spectacular. One had to be five stars' worth of amazing—Augustus Bernstein stars—and one had to be marriage proposal worthy. A month ago, neither of these challenges would be a problem. But now, he had nothing.

Every day, he went into the Stillwater kitchen ready to mix, season, and create and…nothing. Every day he left no closer to his goal, which should have troubled him a lot more than it was.

But instead of thinking about it and pushing through the block, he went to seek out Bria to spend more time with her. A distraction, sure. But a damn beautiful one at that. After that first day on the mountain when he'd kissed her, he'd known she was different. A challenge? Absolutely. The woman was definitely a challenge in the sense that she was wrapped so tightly she hadn't even realized she wanted to kiss him. And she had wanted to kiss him. Her lips had told him that without a doubt. But there was something else, too. Bria was a bit of a mystery to Jax and unlike any woman he'd ever met.

He certainly didn't have her figured out, but dammed if he didn't want to keep trying. Especially if it meant spending more time with her. Which he would be doing shortly, because he'd asked her to come down and try some dishes for him. The problem was, he hadn't made anything yet.

With a sigh, Jax pulled out a chopping board and grabbed the nearest thing—an onion—to start chopping. He needed some inspiration and fast.

"Nice to see you at work."

Jax lifted his head and nodded a greeting to Dylan Harrison. He hadn't seen much of the man lately and Jax knew it was because he was working overtime to make sure everything was in order before the baby was born. By the look of Carmen, it had to be any day, but he was a smart enough man not to tell her that.

"What are you talking about?" Jax replied. "I've been here every day."

Dylan laughed. "I know, I know. No one works harder than you, Jax. I'm just bugging you. But you have to admit, word is you've been spending quite a bit of time with a certain dark-haired guest."

Jax laid down his knife and wiped his hands. "I know you don't like staff and guests dating, but..." He stopped himself. He wasn't dating Bria. He was just helping her out with an assignment. If anything, he was just being a helpful Springs employee. It was definitely not dating. Was it? "Anyway," he continued before Dylan noticed anything wrong. "We're not dating; I'm just helping her out with some pictures."

"Pictures?" Dylan wiggled his eyebrow.

"Not like that, you perv." He threw a towel at his friend and laughed. "She's a photographer and she needed a killer assignment to turn in to her editor, so I suggested she take some pictures of the Springs and—"

"You did what?"

Something in Dylan's voice stopped him and Jax looked up. Dylan did not look impressed. "I suggested she—"

"I heard what you said." Dylan's voice was clipped. "I was wondering why you said it."

Jax didn't know what he'd stepped in, but there was no doubt he'd stepped in something. He searched his friend's face for some kind of clue that he might be kidding. He wasn't. "Look, man, I didn't know it would be a problem. I was just trying to help her out because she had these pictures that....well, it doesn't matter. But I honestly didn't think there was anything wrong with taking pictures of the Springs. I mean, it's good publicity, right?"

Dylan shook his head. "No. It's not."

"I don't understand."

"Ever since we opened, the press has been trying to get in. They want in and we want them out."

"But why? Wouldn't it be good publicity? Free advertising and all that?"

Dylan shook his head, obviously annoyed that Jax wasn't getting it. "No. Not at all. The whole thing with the Springs is that we're an exclusive resort. We're private. We're secluded. Like a retreat. Our guests don't need the whole world knowing their business or where they come to unwind and rejuvenate. And God help us if any of those guests who are here for some kind of treatment have that leaked in the press. Can you imagine the lawsuit? We have some very famous and well-known guests. Part of the appeal is anonymity. We won't sacrifice that. Not for anything."

Jax groaned. "I'm sorry, man. I didn't think of that. I was just trying to help out a—"

"Pretty girl?" Dylan rolled his eyes. "I get it."

Annoyance flared up but Jax pushed it down. He didn't want to help her just because Bria was a pretty girl. Or at least, that's not what it was anymore. Maybe at first, but—hell, he didn't know what it was anymore. But it was definitely something more. "Look, I'm sorry. Her job is on the line so I was just trying to help her out. But, it's fine. I'll talk to her."

Dylan sighed and rolled his shoulders back. "I know you weren't trying to do any harm. But these things have to be run through us. Or Carmen at the very least."

Jax knew his friend was just throwing him a bone, but he appreciated it anyway. And he'd take what he could get because he really didn't want to have to tell Bria she couldn't use the pictures. And the idea of not seeing her every day to work on what he started to think of as *their* project bothered him more than he cared to admit.

"Thanks. I appreciate it."

"No worries. Now tell me, what do you have cooking for your meal with Augustus? It's coming up fast."

Jax groaned but covered it with a smile. "Don't I know it."

BRIA TOOK her time with the last bite of steak, swirling it around the plate and through the peppercorn sauce before finally putting it in her mouth. It was delicious, which was why she'd taken so long to eat it. But she'd eaten every last bite and when she finally looked up, she saw Jax watching her with a bemused expression on his face.

"Enjoy it?"

She shrugged in an effort to look casual. "It was alright."

Jax burst out laughing and spontaneously reached for her hand over the table. She froze for a moment. They'd never shown any kind of affection, or whatever it was, in public before and here they were sitting in the middle of the Stillwater restaurant, Jax's place of employment. As if he read her mind, he gave her hand a squeeze and nodded, so she relaxed.

"It was delicious, Jax." She gestured with her free hand to her empty plate. "Obviously. I can't believe I ate all of it."

"Well, I'm glad you did. And it took you long enough. I've never seen someone take so long to eat before. I was beginning to think you hated it."

"No. The exact opposite. I wanted to enjoy it and make it last. What's the point of having such amazing food prepared for you if you're not going to savor it?"

He smiled his lopsided grin, and her stomach flipped. "Exactly. I'm just happy you liked it."

"I loved it. I think I'd love anything you cooked." Bria could have smacked herself, she sounded so stupid. Like a little girl in love. And she definitely wasn't. In love, that was. It was too soon for anything like that, not that she'd even know hat it felt like. But she was definitely in like. Jax stroked his thumb against the side of her hand and the sensation shot straight to her core. Or lust. Maybe it was lust she was feeling? Whatever it was, she was feeling something.

"I'll have to do it again sometime."

Bria nodded and pulled her hand away, needing some space before she leapt over the table to kiss him. "You said something about needing my help with a decision. What was that?"

His face clouded over; his eyes darkened automatically before he could hide it. "It's nothing," he said quickly. She was no mind reader, but Bria was smart enough to know it was something. "I was going to cook you a few different dishes to see which one you liked the best, but I decided not to."

She could tell there was more to it than that, but she didn't push. He'd tell her if he wanted to. It wasn't as if he owed her any kind of explanation or anything. They weren't dating. They were just…well, Bria didn't know exactly what they were doing. But they definitely weren't dating.

"Well, like I said. Anytime you want to cook for me, I'm not going to turn you down." She smiled and soon the light came back into his eyes and whatever it was that had been bothering him was gone.

"I'd love to," he said. "Tell me what your favorite foods are."

The question caught her off guard and she sat back in her chair. "I've never been asked that before."

"Never?"

She didn't want to tell him that her parents had been too busy to care about things like that, and even if she'd told them, they likely would have made some comment about it not being important and brushed it off. They'd moved so much when Bria was so young, she didn't have any real friends who would have cared about her favorite things and whenever she did hang out with Kristie, they usually grabbed whatever was fast and easy, which usually meant some sort of noodle from some-place. Maybe her grandma knew, but—

"Bria?"

She shook her head and focused on Jax, who watched her closely.

"It wasn't a hard question," he said. "You don't know what your favorite foods are? Really?"

"I like fish."

He laughed. "Fish? Any type specifically?"

"I don't know. Honestly, you probably think this is crazy,

but I haven't given it much thought. Ever. I just eat when I'm hungry and I know what I like. I really liked that steak."

"So steak is your favorite?"

"No." She smiled. "I told you, fish."

He laughed again, and Bria joined him. It was so easy to be herself with him. In fact, to be someone she didn't even know was herself. She'd never felt so carefree and light before, but just being with Jax made her feel as if everything would be okay and somehow things would all work out. "If I was given a choice on a menu, I'd pick fish."

"Okay," he said, suddenly serious again. "Why? What is it about fish that you like?"

She thought for a minute because the question was obviously important to him. "I know this will sounds stupid," she said after a moment. "But it's like fish can be anything you want it to be."

He seemed to consider what she said. "Interesting point. There's not a lot of fish around here, but we do have access to some pretty fresh salmon and trout from the lakes and rivers. I'll make you fish next time. But I'd also really like to cook you some of the local flavors like venison and—no?"

Bria tried to relax her face because she was pretty certain he'd seen some uncertainty there. It's not that she didn't like wild meat; she'd just never had it before. But if anyone was to cook it so she enjoyed it, she had a feeling it would be Jax.

It was her turn to reach across the table and take his hand. She flipped it over and ran a finger down his wrist into his palm before she threaded her fingers through his. "You know what? If you're the one cooking it, I know I'd love it."

DID the woman have any idea how simple words could drive him crazy? No. Clearly she didn't. Or if she did, she was enjoying every second of it. He squeezed her hand. He would have liked to do a whole lot more, but they were in his place of employment and even though Dylan had never gotten around to saying that he couldn't see Bria, Jax was pretty sure it wouldn't be a good idea to jump over the table and kiss the woman within half an inch of ecstasy. So he restrained himself.

But all those feelings dried up when Bria said, "So when do I get to take pictures of the kitchen?"

Damn. He needed to tell her what Dylan had said. But how was he going to basically crush her hopes for the photo spread that was going to save her career? What if she blamed him? Worse, what if she didn't want to spend time with him anymore and was only with him to get the shots? The thought bothered him a lot more than he cared to admit. He'd never let a woman get to him this way; he needed to shake it off.

Bria was still talking. "I think they'll be great shots. People love to see the behind the scenes of where amazing food is prepared and if I can get in—"

He stopped her despite everything in him wanting to do anything but. If he could, Jax would keep her talking about her photos and he'd sit all night and watch the way she lit up when she got excited about her pictures. It was the sexiest thing he'd ever seen and the only time he'd ever really seen her totally let go and forget to censor herself with whatever internal checks and balances she usually had going on that kept her so in control. He didn't know what it was, or why it was she insisted on keeping her walls so high, but he sure enjoyed watching them come down bit by bit. And if he could only get her alone for a little while, he'd be sure to bring them all the way down.

But it wasn't the time to think about bringing Bria's walls down, or anything else on Bria down. He needed to focus on breaking the news to her that he'd screwed up. Bad.

When he didn't immediately say anything else, Bria asked, "What is it? Was I boring you with all my picture talk? I know it can be boring for anyone who isn't as in to photography as I am. Hell, for anyone else, really. But I can't help it. I haven't been so excited for a project since...well...since ever." She laughed and the sound he'd only heard a few times before hit him in the gut as if she'd punched him. Telling her was going to be harder than he'd thought. A lot harder.

He ran a hand through his hair before he took hers in his. "Bria, I know you're really excited about this project, and I can't even begin to tell you how much I like watching you talk about the pictures, take the shots and...well, you are pretty sexy with that camera." He smiled at the memory of her the night before as she took shots of the fountain at the front door lit for the night. It was beyond sexy the way she handled that camera with such authority. He couldn't help but wonder what else she'd handle with that much authority. Again, he shook his head. It wasn't the time or the place to think about those kinds of things.

She smiled, and the look in her eyes made it clear she was following along with exactly what he was saying.

"I'm glad you like watching because I have a lot more pictures to take and with the way this is going, I just know Kristie's going to love it. She might even want a whole different spread. Maybe I can—"

He shook his head, which both served to clear his head from the image of Bria with her camera and stop her from talking. Again. "But that's not what I need to tell you." He squeezed her hand a little. "Bria, we need to talk."

Instantly her face changed as she noticed the change in his voice. "Jax, what? Why do you look so serious?"

"I'm so sorry, Bria." He shook his head and deciding it wasn't worth putting it off any longer, he decided to just say it. "You can't use the pictures, Bria."

"What?"

"You can't use the pictures. They won't allow it."

"Who? What are you talking about?" She pulled her hand away from his and sat back against the seat. "Jax, you're not making any sense. Who won't let me use the pictures?"

"Dylan and Trent Harrison. They own the Springs and they won't let you use the pictures. I'm sorry, I should have run it by them first."

"That doesn't make any sense. Why wouldn't they want them? It's free advertising and the publicity will be fantastic. Just think—when people see the pictures of how amazing the rooms are and maybe even a glimpse of some of the guests, and the type of celebrity that the resort attracts, they're going to be lining up to stay here."

"That's exactly what they don't want."

"They don't want people lining up to stay in the resort?" Bria crossed her arms and glared at him in challenge. "That's the stupidest thing I've ever heard."

"No." He wanted to reach for her hand again, but by the look of her, she was definitely not going to offer it up anytime soon. "Look, it's my fault I didn't ask and that I encouraged you at the beginning and everything. But really I'm just the messenger in all of this. Don't be mad at me."

As he said the words, he realized just how strongly he didn't want her to be mad at him. Because if she blamed him, this— whatever *this* was—would be over. And he knew he didn't want it to be over. Not when it had hardly begun. Not when he hadn't had the chance to run his hands down her naked body and held those two perfect breasts that he knew without a doubt would fit perfectly in each of his hands without the cover of the cotton t-shirts Bria favored. Not when he hadn't had a chance to watch her beautiful face transform in ecstasy as he brought her to climax. No. Whatever it was that was going on between them was definitely not going to be over until that happened. At the very least.

"Bria. Talk to me."

Her lips were pressed into a tight line and Jax couldn't even begin to read her expression.

Finally, without warning, her face crumpled and he thought she might even cry. He wouldn't have blamed her if she did. After all, these pictures were important to her. She didn't cry and he was secretly very glad. One thing he couldn't handle was a weepy woman. Her shoulders slumped and she released her hands, letting them fall on the table.

Jax didn't hesitate. He reached for her hand and gripped it tight. "Look at me."

She did.

"I know this isn't what you wanted to hear, but don't cry. Please."

To his surprise, she snorted. A move that was exceptionally cute, but he was smart enough not to mention it. "I'm not going to cry over some pictures, Jax. Yes, I'm upset." She sighed and looked down at the table. "I'm really upset." She tried to yank her hand away again, but he pulled back and forced her to look up. "I'm not going to lie. This is not good. Not good at all. I need those photos. I promised a behind-the-scenes exclusive. There's a lot riding on this. A lot."

The brief moment of relief that she wasn't going to cry was overshadowed by her obvious distress. In all the time they'd spent together, it hadn't occurred to Jax that he might actually start to care about her more than just a challenge to be conquered. But to his surprise, he did. A lot.

"Can you just sell them on a different story? Maybe something about the town?'

She shook her head. "No way. You don't understand. It's complicated, but if I don't turn this assignment in, I'll lose my job."

"You can't use the pictures, Bria. They'll take legal action."

She hung her head. "I know."

They sat in silence for a second. Jax wanted so badly to fix the whole screw-up, but knew he couldn't.

Or maybe he could.

"Maybe you could use some of the pictures? What if you showed them the pictures and they approved them before you submitted them?" He had no idea if that would work, or even if either of the Harrisons would go for it. But if he had to, he'd use some of his personal sway, for whatever it was worth anyway.

"They won't agree to that."

"They might."

They would. He'd make sure of it.

"I guess it's worth a try," she finally agreed.

It was worth more than a try. And from the tentative smile she gave him, Jax knew it was worth a whole lot more than just a try.

Chapter Seven

AFTER JAX DROPPED his bomb on her about the photos, she'd gone through a lot of feelings. Most of which involved anger and defeat. Her initial reaction was to be pissed at Jax. After all, the whole thing was his idea. If it hadn't been for him, she wouldn't have gotten her hopes up and spent so much time on a project that would go nowhere. But she also wouldn't have had one of the best weeks in recent memory, and been able to spend so much time with him. Time she'd enjoyed a lot more than she was ready to admit.

It wasn't Jax's fault. And he had tried to help, which is why she was waiting to speak to Carmen. Jax had set up the meeting for her, even though she'd hoped to meet with the Harrison brothers, who owned the resort and would make the ultimate decision. But apparently they were both busy with other meetings, and Bria would take what she could get. Besides, Jax told her that if she could get Carmen on her side, it would hold a lot of sway with the brothers.

And hell, if the woman had that much sway over the owners of the resort, one of which was her boyfriend, it was worth a shot to win her over. And Bria was determined to do her best. Especially considering her first few run-ins with her hadn't been entirely positive.

In an effort to be prepared as possible, Bria had run down to town and begged Cynthia to print out the pictures in a hurry for her. She'd flipped through them quickly and pulled out any pictures that clearly weren't going to work. Like the ones of Jax she'd taken when he hadn't been looking. His strong profile silhouetted by the setting sun was hot. More than hot, it emphasized a stillness about Jax that she only saw once in a while. Kind of an introspective quiet that made her want to learn more about him. More than how his lips felt on hers. And she already knew she liked that. A lot.

When Cynthia handed her the packet of photos, she hadn't said a word about those shots, but Bria knew the other woman had seen them by the narrowed look she'd given her. Undoubtedly, Cynthia would have noticed the intimacy that was implied by them. Little did she know that the level of intimacy between Bria and Jax hadn't gone any further than a stolen kiss whenever they were away from the Springs, or thought no one might be looking. But Bria had a feeling that wouldn't matter to the other woman. Not when Cynthia clearly had some sort of feelings for Jax.

But so did she. She just couldn't seem to figure out what they were. She tucked the pictures of Jax in a side pocket of her bag. All she really knew was that their stolen kisses were growing in intensity, and despite every reason she shouldn't, Bria desperately wanted that sexy mouth of Jax's in more places than her lips.

She smoothed her hair and tried to force the images that particular thought brought to mind. There would be time for those thoughts later and maybe—

No. She had to focus.

Bria rapped on the office door and to her surprise, it opened almost at once.

"Oh." Carmen, looking more pregnant than Bria actually thought was possible, stood on the other side of the door, her face flushed.

"Hi. I'm not early, am I?"

"No." Carmen waved her hand in front of her face. "I was just...is it hot in here?"

Bria shook her head slowly. "Are you okay? You look a little—"

"It's hot in here. You don't think so?"

"I'm fine," Bria said. "Did you want to..." She was going to suggest they reschedule because Carmen didn't look as though she was in any state to have a conversation, let alone one so important to Bria, but rescheduling wasn't an option. Bria was running out of time. "I just have a few pictures to show you," she said instead. "They won't take long to look at, and I think you'll like—"

"Let's walk."

"But...the pictures?"

"We'll look while we walk." Carmen started toward Bria, who still stood in the doorway. She quickly darted out of the way when Carmen didn't show any sign of slowing down. There was no way they were both going to fit in the small space.

Carmen didn't wait for Bria to catch up, but walked down the hallway at a pace that seemed excessively fast for someone of such girth. Bria didn't have a lot of experience with pregnant women. Or any at all, really, but she did think it unusual and impressive that Carmen could move so quickly. Jax had said something about her being close to her due date. To Bria, she looked as if she must be at least a month overdue. How was it even possible for the human body to stretch so much? She tried not to stare but it was impossible not to.

"Carmen," Bria said as she caught up. "I know this probably isn't the best time, but—"

"Of course it's a good time." She smiled, but it looked pained. "My to-do list seems to be growing instead of shrinking, I haven't found anyone suitable to replace me when I take some time off, Dylan is stuck in meetings with investors for the next few days, and I'm going to have a baby any day now that I'm not even remotely prepared for. Today is as good a time as any."

If she had any other choice, Bria would have used that moment to excuse herself and get as far away from Carmen and her obvious hormone overload as possible. But she didn't have any other choice. Carmen, in her overworked, hormonal glory, was the only choice she had. She took a deep breath and pushed on, determined to at least get the meeting over with as soon as possible.

"Well, maybe taking a quick look at these pictures will help take one thing off your plate." She reached into her bag and pulled out the packet of photos.

Carmen slowed her pace a little bit and took the pictures but didn't look at them right away. "Look, Bria, I know I said I'd look at them. Jax all but begged me to give you a chance with this."

Bria felt a little tug in her gut at that. Jax really did care about this. And her. She shook her head. That didn't matter.

"But," Carmen continued, "I really don't think we can allow these shots to be used." She held up the photos, but still hadn't looked at them. "Part of the appeal of the Springs is—oh."

Carmen came to an abrupt stop while she stared at the photo, and Bria had to catch herself before she either walked into Carmen or the nearby fountain. She turned quickly to see Carmen stare down at the picture in her hand. Bria tried to hold her excitement in check. She might not like the shots. She might like them but reject them anyway. She held her breath and waited while Carmen quickly flipped through the stack.

Occasionally she paused and looked at one image longer than the others, but she didn't say another word.

It couldn't have taken long. Maybe only a minute or two, but to Bria it felt like an eternity. Finally, she took a chance. "What do you think?"

Carmen looked up and smiled. It was the first time since their meeting started that Bria had seen her look like the calm and put together woman she knew Carmen was. "I think you have an amazing eye. These are good. Really good."

Bria waited, knowing there would be a "but."

"I don't think we can use all of them."

There it was. *Wait.*

"What? All of them? Does that mean you can use some of them?" She couldn't help it; she got her hopes up. If she could use even some of the pictures, it would be better than nothing and Bria was almost positive she could convince Kristie that it would be just as good. Almost positive. But she'd figure that part out if it came to that. For the moment, she was focused on Carmen and the hope the woman had given her. "Even if I could use a few, I'd make sure that—"

Carmen laughed and held up a hand. "Don't get ahead of yourself. But I really think Dylan was probably a bit rash in his decision to say no photos at all. And if he saw these, he would absolutely see what I see and that's an incredible eye for detail. You've managed to catch the feeling of the hot pools without actually showing them in this one."

The picture she referred to was taken when Jax had shown her the pool area. It was spectacular, with a few large pools of different temperatures for all the guests to soak or swim in, and the area that made the Springs really special—the private pools. They were hidden among lush, almost tropical foliage, giving the guests a private soaking experience. She'd focused on shooting the atmosphere of the room: the mist, the plants, the way the water burbled.

"We can use images like these, and I don't see why Dylan or Trent would have any objection to that because it doesn't really give anything away. They're almost like art."

That was as close to permission as she was going to get and while it would be much better if she could get it in writing, for the moment, Bria would take it. "So I can use them?"

Carmen nodded. "I think—oh!"

This time Carmen was definitely not exclaiming over the pictures she held in her hand. And she didn't hold them in her hand at all. The photos scattered all over the floor as Carmen abandoned them to clutch her swollen belly.

"Are you..." Bria looked around for someone, anyone who could help out but of course no one milled around. "Carmen? Are you okay?"

Carmen was curled around her stomach as best as she could be from her standing position. Her breaths came harder and faster, and her eyes were squeezed tightly shut. There was no way Carmen could be in labor, was there? She hadn't actually told Bria when she was due, but surely it couldn't be today. She wouldn't have taken a meeting if she was due to have a baby.

"Is the baby due today?"

Carmen shook her head and struggled to straighten up. Her face was covered in a sheen of sweat. "No," she managed to say. "Not for another few days."

Bria breathed a sigh of relief. "Well, that's good. For a second, I was worried that—"

Carmen grabbed her hand and squeezed so hard, the pain cut off the rest of her thought. "I think..." Carmen let out a series of short breaths. "I'm in..." She gripped Bria's hand tighter. "Labor." She managed to push the last word out.

"But you said—" Bria didn't bother to finish her sentence when Carmen snapped her head up and glared at her. "Okay. Why don't we get you to sit down?"

Bria was way out of her league with a laboring woman. She'd never known anyone who'd had a baby. Not well anyway. There'd been a few women in the office, or acquaintances who had babies, but she hadn't known them well and she certainly hadn't been there when someone had gone through it. Wasn't that why there were due dates? To predict these things so you could stay home and get ready? Bria racked her brain for something to do. She needed to find help. Someone who was much more prepared to handle such a thing.

She led Carmen to a nearby bench right as another contraction seized the woman. Bria did her best not to squeal when Carmen squeezed her hand again. The woman had incredible grip strength and Bria was going to have to find her something else to squish if Bria was going to escape with her bones intact.

"Sit here," Bria instructed. "I'm going to find—"

"No." Carmen reached out and pulled her down in front of her. "Don't leave me," she growled, as if the sweet woman had been taken over by a demonic predator.

"I'm not going to…" She trailed off. Lying to a woman in Carmen's condition was probably not the best idea. "I just need to find you someone who can—"

"No."

"Okay." She said the word slowly, completely unsure of what to do next. "I'll call Dylan for you then. What's his number?"

"I don't have—" Another contraction gripped her and Carmen was lost in the moment.

Bria found herself naturally breathing through it and tried to get Carmen to follow suit. "Breathe. One…two…" To her surprise, it worked and Carmen slowed her breaths, matched the rhythm Bria was somehow setting. When the contraction passed, Bria stood and once again scanned the hall for someone. She certainly didn't know much about what was going on, but it was clear Carmen was going to have a baby and from the look of things, soon.

Her eyes locked on a familiar figure at the end of the hall, and she called out, "Grandma!"

Mona heard her and turned, a smile on her face as she made her way toward them. "Bria, what are—" She took in the scene in front of her. "Carmen?"

"She's in labor," Bria said. "But it's not her due date. I don't know—"

Mona looked at her sharply. "You do know that babies don't arrive on a schedule." Bria nodded dumbly. Sure, she should have known that, but it didn't make any sense to have an actual date if it didn't mean anything. She knew enough not to get into that debate at that moment.

"We have to get her to a hospital," her grandma announced.

Once again, Bria tried to make her escape. "I'll go find—"

"No. Stay with me." Carmen looked up at her. The other woman's eyes were dark with fear. As much as Bria wanted to get away, she couldn't leave Carmen. Not like that.

"I'm not going anywhere." She gave Carmen the most reassuring smile she could muster. "Now breathe with me. One...two..."

JAX WAS BARELY inside the sliding doors of Cedar Springs General Hospital when he heard the group of people gathered in the waiting room. With a smile on his face, he walked straight into the thick of it and smacked Trent on the back.

"I assume a congratulations is in order, Uncle."

His friend had such a big smile on his face, Jax had to laugh. "Thanks, buddy. I can't wait to meet the little guy."

"It's a boy? That's awesome."

"His name's Hunter Dylan and he was…" Trent turned to his girlfriend Samantha for help.

"Seven pounds, eight ounces, and twenty-one inches long. A big healthy boy," she provided with a smile.

Trent shrugged. "Details."

"I hear ya. Well, congratulations again." Jax slapped Trent on the back one more time and let him get back to talking with the other well-wishers.

He felt better now that he knew everyone was healthy and the baby was okay. Up until that moment, all he knew was that Carmen had gone into labor quickly and had been rushed to the hospital, with Bria holding her hand before Dylan could even be pulled out of his meeting. Mona had filled him when he was done with the lunch service, and he'd rushed down to the hospital as soon as he could. And by the looks of it, so had every single person Carmen and Dylan knew in Cedar Springs. Including Rhys Anderson, who was still in his uniform.

"You're not still on shift, are you?"

Rhys shrugged. "It's a slow day. I heard the call come over the radio, so I used a little police power to get Dylan down the mountain quickly."

"Did everyone in town hear about it on the radio? I thought hospitals were supposed to be quiet?" Jax joked.

"They are." Rhys looked over his shoulder. "We've already been warned once. I think pretty soon this party will have to move down to the Grizzly Paw. Besides, they won't let anyone in to see them anyway, so there's no point sticking around. Did you come down here just to join the party?"

Sure, Jax was happy for his friends, but that wasn't the real reason he'd shown up. "Of course," he lied and winked at Rhys as he searched the room for the one person he really wanted to see.

"She's over there." Rhys pointed subtly to a corner. "By the soda machine."

"How did you—"

"Word travels fast in a small town." Rhys shrugged. "Kari tried to invite her over to join us, but she didn't want any part of it." Kari Fox was the love of Rhys's life and knew exactly what it was like to be new to town and the group of friends. Jax wasn't surprised that Bria hadn't wanted to join them. They were an intimidating group at the best of times, let alone when you were someone like Bria.

And what kind of someone was that? Someone he wanted to spend time alone with, that was for sure.

Rhys elbowed him in the ribs. "She's hot. But she seems a little—"

"Don't say it, man." Jax reflexively curled his fingers into a fist, not that he'd actually hit the officer. Besides the fact that he was a cop, he was also his friend. But he also wouldn't let anyone say anything remotely negative about Bria. His protectiveness surprised him but he shook it off.

"Hey, settle down." Rhys held his hands up in mock surrender and laughed. "I was just going to say that she seems a little stunned. I heard she came in with Carmen. I didn't know they knew each other. She's a guest at the Springs, right?"

Jax nodded, but didn't feel like getting into details. Especially considering he didn't have all of them himself. "I should..." He started to give some sort of lame explanation, but drifted off when he realized he didn't care. He only cared about getting to Bria, who looked totally out of place and—Rhys was right—a little stunned as she sat in the corner of the busy room. Jax walked away from Rhys without another word and crossed the room.

"Hey there."

Bria jerked her head up, obviously shocked by his voice. "Hi."

"I hear you're quite the hero." He sat on the chair next to her, but refrained from touching her in any way. He didn't need to give his friends anything else to gossip about.

She shook her head, her eyes not focusing on anything. "I've never seen anything like that. She was in so much pain and…" Bria held her hand up for Jax to inspect. It was swollen and the faint outline of a purple bruise appeared on the top. Fortunately it was her left hand and wouldn't affect her taking pictures.

Forgetting his friends, who probably watched them with interest, he took her hand gently in his own and kissed it. "I know Carmen was strong, but…wow."

"She was screaming and—well, not really screaming. More of a wailing sound. And she'd squeeze my hand and…" She turned to look at him then. "I've never seen anything like it. She wouldn't let me leave. I kept trying to go and find her a friend, or someone who would be better at it than I was, but…"

Jax reached out and smoothed her hair back from her face. "You did great, Bria." He didn't know any of the details, but there was no doubt that this feisty, strong-willed woman who he was growing more and more fond of, rose to the challenge of helping Carmen through her labor. No doubt in his mind. "Why don't we get out of here?"

She nodded in relief. "Please."

Jax helped her up and put his arm protectively around her shoulders. He warded off any comment or attempt at conversation from his friends by avoiding eye contact completely and steered Bria quickly around the crowd and out the door.

Chapter Eight

ONCE SHE GOT out in the fresh air, Bria perked up quickly. And it didn't hurt to have Jax at her side as they rode in the truck. His proximity affected her in a totally different way, but one that at least didn't shock her into a zombie state the way she'd been since she'd left Carmen's hospital room. She'd been lucky to get out of there right before the woman began to push. It'd been bad enough listening to her cry out in pain while she squeezed her hand until she thought all the bones would either shatter or just meld together as one. Never mind all the other invasive and somewhat gory things she'd had to witness just by being in the room. She shuddered at the memory. If that's what childbirth was like, she wanted no part of it, in any capacity.

"Feeling better?"

She looked over to see Jax watch her with a smile on his face.

"I've never seen anyone react that way to labor."

"And you've seen a lot of people who've experienced that, have you?"

Jax shrugged. "Not really. But I thought that type of thing came naturally to women."

"Not this woman." Bria had never been the overly nurturing type and she'd certainly never been anyone's labor coach before. One thing was for sure: it most certainly had not come naturally.

Jax chuckled. "You never fail to surprise me, Bria."

"Because I'm not naturally nurturing?"

"No," he said quite seriously. "Because you don't realize how amazing you are. And how incredibly sexy you look right now."

Normally she would have shrugged off the compliment but after the afternoon she'd just had, Bria let his words soak in and warm her. She'd never felt as beautiful and so completely confident as she did with Jax, and even after everything she'd just been through with Carmen, the only thing on her mind was Jax and the way her body felt as though it was on fire when he was near. She'd had enough of dancing around it. Without overthinking it, she undid her seatbelt and slid across the bench seat so she was pressed up against his side with her hand resting on his denim-clad thigh. The muscles under her fingers twitched in response to the touch, which only encouraged Bria to slide her fingers down and around his leg, squeezing a little as she moved.

Jax let out a groan and wrapped his right arm around her, giving her a squeeze. "You're killing me, Bria. I'm trying to drive here."

"Don't let me stop you," she teased, hardly even believing the boldness coming out of her. Only twenty minutes ago, she was ready to pass out from exhaustion, and now with the heat of Jax's body beneath her hands, sleep was the furthest thing from her mind.

He groaned again, and with a jerk of his hand on the steering wheel, pulled off on a side road.

"Where are we going?"

"You'll see." His voice was deep, gruff, and barely contained.

While he drove over the road that continued to get rougher, the truck bounced and jostled her on the seat, but Bria used the motion as an excuse to let her hands wander freely over his leg, and up to his crotch of his jeans that strained from the growing erection they contained. A smile of satisfaction that Bria could have such an effect on him so quickly crossed her lips and growing bolder still, she walked her fingers up to his waistband and the button of his jeans.

As Bria pushed the button through the hole of the denim, and slowly, tortuously, pulled down the zipper, Jax pressed down on the accelerator, pushed the truck to drive as fast on the rough gravel road as he could safely manage.

"God, Bria." He sucked in a gasp of air as she reached into his pants and pulled his throbbing cock free.

This time when she smiled, it was out of pure satisfaction from what she saw. Jax was impressive, the way she knew he would be. Her own anticipation built as she wrapped her hand around him, and his body trembled under her grip. Bria knew she was torturing him, teasing him beyond reason, but the sense of power she held over him was heady and she wanted more.

Now both his hands gripped the steering wheel, and when Bria stole a glance, she saw his knuckles were white with concentrated effort as he navigated the truck down the road. She rose up, keeping one hand firmly in place, and trailed soft kisses from his earlobe, moving slowly down his neck.

"Bria, I…"

"Yes?" Her voice was laced with innocence, but there was nothing sweet about her intentions.

"You're going to—"

He was silenced when Bria once again returned her attention to his crotch, this time taking him in her mouth.

THE WOMAN WAS GOING to kill them, or at least him with that hot little mouth of hers working magic he couldn't even comprehend in his lap. It took all the willpower Jax had to focus on the road, lest he drive into a tree and end their afternoon rendezvous before it even began.

They were almost there. Not that it would matter if Bria kept doing that... "Oh God, Bria." He took one hand off the wheel and threaded his fingers through her hair. "You're going to need to—"

"What?" She lifted her head long enough for him to see the mischief in her eyes. She had no intention of stopping. That much was clear by the way she promptly ignored his halfhearted protests and returned to her task.

And they were halfhearted because dammed if he didn't want her to keep doing exactly what she was doing. But he also wanted to do a whole lot more, and if she didn't slow down, he'd be done before he had a chance to really get started.

Thankfully, moments later his turn appeared, and he yanked the steering wheel hard to the left and onto the even narrower trail that led to their final destination. The movement of the truck momentarily distracted Bria, but it didn't take long before her hands were back on him, trailing down the inside of his thigh, causing a million nerve endings to fire all through his body.

"If I didn't know better, I'd think you did that on purpose." She smiled up at him and he laughed.

"Trust me, baby. There is nothing I want more than that sweet mouth of yours all over me. Except to have mine on you." He steered the truck around a boulder and off the road into a small pull-out. "And that's exactly what's going to happen." He slammed the gearshift into park, undid his seatbelt and grabbed Bria's waist, all with surprising speed. But after all, he was a man on a mission, and that mission involved having Bria's hot little mouth on his, and his cock deep inside her.

"I think it's my turn," he whispered in her ear as he tugged her onto his lap. There was no objection from Bria as she straddled him. He put one hand on the back of her head and pulled her down to him, meeting her mouth with a hunger that had been building for far too long. More than anything, he wanted to take his time with her, savor every inch of her body with his mouth. But that would have to wait. There would be time for slow and sensual later. He needed to be inside this woman. Now.

As his mouth explored hers, his tongue tangling with hers, Jax let his hands slide down to the buttons of her blouse. Too impatient to fumble with the delicate buttons, he took the fabric in both hands and pulled, popping the buttons, and revealed the silk of her black lacy bra beneath. She pulled away from their kiss to let out a deep moan and Jax could feel her quiver with need against him.

He focused his attention to her breasts, just barely covered by the sexy lace of her bra. He sucked one nipple into his mouth, not bothering to move the lace out of the way, while his other hand kneaded her other breast. His thumb flicked against her nipple until it too was a firm peak under his touch.

"Those jeans have got to go." Jax looked into her eyes, dark with need.

There were no objections from Bria as she half stood as well as she could in the cab. Jax reached out and undid the buttons of her jeans, pushed the denim down over her hips. While she shimmied the rest of the way out of her pants, Jax took care of the details of the condom, and divested himself of his own jeans.

Moments later, he had his hands on her bare hips and pulled her down and on top of him in one strong move. He stared directly in her eyes so he didn't miss the slight flinch as he filled her before her pupils dilated completely as passion flooded through her. She dropped her head back, exposed her long throat and gave herself over to their union. It was the sexiest thing Jax had ever seen, and he met her need hard and fast. His hands returned to her breasts as they both quickly rode to their peaks.

It was fast and hard and the best damn sex he'd had in years. Listening to Bria cry out with pure abandon as she climaxed clinched his own orgasm. When finally she collapsed over him and rested on his shoulder, he wrapped his arms around her and held her tight as her breathing returned to normal.

Things between them were only supposed to be temporary. Hell, everything with Jax was temporary. But as he held her, felt her heart beat against his chest, there was one thing Jax knew for certain—whatever had just happened between them, he definitely wanted it to happen again.

Chapter Nine

IN ANOTHER LIFE, Bria would have been embarrassed after what they'd just done in his truck out in public, where anyone could see. Anyone who happened to be on a remote mountain road, anyway. Or at least she would have been a little awkward afterwards. But she didn't feel any of those things. How could she when she'd just had the most amazing sex of her life and Jax looked at her as if he was ready to devour her all over again?

There was nothing awkward about it at all. Well, except the fact that her shirt had been destroyed and she wore Jax's t-shirt knotted at her waist. Her body flushed with the memory of Jax's impatience with her blouse. Never had she been with a man so unbelievably eager to get to her that he didn't have the patience to take her clothing off.

It made her feel wanted, desirable, and so incredibly sexy. Jax did that to her.

She hadn't even realized where he'd parked the truck or where he'd taken her until she'd finally been able to pull herself together and join him outside. The sun had set while they were *busy* and Bria kept forgetting how quickly it got dark once the sun dropped below the mountains. She made her way around the truck where Jax waited and was about to tug her hair into an elastic and get the tangle of dark locks off her shoulders, but Jax stopped her.

"No." He pulled the elastic out of her hand and used his fingers to shake out her hair. "I like it down." He kissed her then, one hand still threaded through her hair, leaving her breathless before he released her. "Are you ready? I have something to show you."

"Ready for what? It's pitch black out here."

"I come prepared." He flicked on a flashlight. Bria could see he had a backpack slung over one shoulder and he extended his other hand out to her. She took it and fell into step next to him.

"I wasn't really prepared for this little stop." He winked and the heat of the memory of what she'd done in the truck flooded through her. "But I usually have a few things in the box of my truck and there's no better time than now."

"For what?"

"To show you the midnight springs."

She'd forgotten he'd promised to take her back to the natural hot springs that were hidden deep in the mountains at night. Of course, when he'd made the promise, she hadn't really expected him to follow through on it. In fact, she hadn't really expected any of what had just happened to happen. So really, all bets were off.

"I forgot all about that."

He stopped and stared at her with such intensity that she almost had to look away. "I didn't."

THE HIKE to the springs didn't take long because they'd driven most of the way up, but the pools were still tucked a little bit off the rustic road. Bria's flats weren't really meant for the trails, let alone trails in the dark, so she was careful to pick her way through the rocks and roots. The last thing she needed was to sprain an ankle as well as have a swollen hand. The pain in her hand had been forgotten with their earlier activities, but it had started to throb with a constant reminder that it was still there and still very sore.

Once they arrived, Jax laid out a blanket and lit some candles that did a good job illuminating their space. The pools bubbled next to them, and the heat coming from the water was enough to warm the air around them. Bria desperately wanted to slip into their warm, soothing waters and soak the day away, but her stomach growled with hunger. First things first.

Jax spread out his picnic, which comprised of a can of soda, two granola bars, and half a box of crackers, and they settled in to enjoy their feast. Bria sat on the opposite side of the blanket from him, not because she needed space, but because she was pretty sure they wouldn't be able to have any conversation if they were any closer—she wouldn't be able to keep her hands off him. Now that they'd crossed that line, there was no going back and despite the fact that Bria logically knew things between them were temporary while she was visiting, she didn't care. She was in absolutely no hurry to go back to the way things were. A small taste of Jax wasn't enough. She wanted more and by the way he looked at her, so did he.

"This is a lovely dinner, thank you." She tried not to laugh as she broke a piece of cracker off and popped it in her mouth. "You really know how to impress."

"Hey, you should be impressed I had anything in my truck at all."

"Trust me, I am."

He winked at her, and Bria's whole body responded with the simple action. "You didn't ask how the meeting with Carmen went," she said, changing the subject.

"She got a healthy baby boy out of it, so I'm thinking it

went pretty well." He passed her the can of soda and slid a little closer to her on the blanket. "It must have been pretty successful."

"Well, I actually think it was. Aside from the whole baby thing." She waved her hand, dismissing the one major development that came from the meeting. "She liked the photos." Well, she'd liked them before she dropped them on the ground and curled around her belly anyway. For the first time, Bria wondered what might have happened to those pictures. Her grandmother must have picked them up. She wouldn't have just left them there. Anyway, it didn't matter; they were just prints.

"Did she say anything about actually using the pictures?" Jax slid a little closer still until his hand was on her thigh. He trailed his fingers up her leg, stopping just shy of where her body had already begun to react to his touch.

Bria resolutely ignored him. She made a show of taking another cracker and breaking it into pieces before she put it in her mouth. All the while, Jax's fingers continued their exploration, inched their way up her body so they were on the bare skin of her stomach, and then farther still so they traced the outline of her breasts. When he reached up and cupped her breast, squeezing with just enough pressure to make her gasp, she finally dropped the cracker and the pretense of ignoring him.

"I thought we were talking."

"We are. But I also would really like to do this."

Jax crawled up over her on the blanket until he covered her, with his body hovering just above hers. She could smell the unique mixture of manliness and something else, some yummy lingering scent from the kitchen, that clung to the sweatshirt he'd found in his truck when he gave her his t-shirt.

"I thought we came to see the springs," she protested, but her heart was definitely not in it.

"We did." He kissed her on the lips and sucked her bottom lip up gently as he pulled back again. "And we will. But first I'm going to kiss you all over, taste every inch of your body, and make you scream while you look up at the stars and feel like you're among them. And then, when you come back to earth, I'm going to take you slowly until you beg me for release again." She shivered under him, her body already silently begging him. "And then when we're both satisfied, we'll slip into the water and do it all over again."

"Is that a promise?"

His grin was wicked in the candlelight before he brought his mouth to her belly while his hands worked the buttons on her jeans. He looked up, his eyes meeting hers with a flash of desire. "Absolutely."

BY THE TIME Jax finally and quite reluctantly dropped Bria off at her room, he should have been exhausted, but he wasn't. Far from it. He was wide awake. Every nerve ending in his body buzzed with the evening he'd just had. It was well after two in the morning, but there was no way he was going to be able to sleep. Even if Bria was beside him, there would be no sleep. Hell, especially if Bria was beside him. Now that he'd had her, she was all he wanted.

Never before had a woman been like a drug he couldn't get enough of. Sure, he'd had good lovers in the past. He'd had exceptional lovers, but none of them came close to the way Bria's entire body shuddered underneath him when he brought her to climax, the way she arched her back, the way—damn, he needed to stop replaying it or before he knew it, he'd be banging down her door.

Which wasn't a half bad idea, really. But he didn't think it would earn him any points with Bria's grandmother, and besides that, Bria needed to sleep. He'd like to take complete credit for her total exhaustion, but it wasn't just their lovemaking—it was also the emotional toll the day had taken with Carmen and the baby.

He'd give her time to sleep, but he sure as hell wasn't going to leave her alone for long. Not with the memory of the way her mouth had felt on him, and the bold way she'd crossed the barrier between them, fresh in his mind. He knew she was feisty, and he wasn't an idiot; he'd felt the sexual tension between them building, too. But she'd shocked the hell out of him with her move in his truck.

With a shake of his head, Jax left Bria's room and headed down to the only place he could think to go when he was wired. The kitchen. He'd been putting things off long enough and it was time he at least figured things out for Slade and Beth. His friends deserved the best and dammit if he wasn't going to give it to them.

The kitchen was quiet and dark. It would still be a few hours before anyone came in to start the morning baking, so he had the place to himself. He flipped the radio on, preferring to work with classic rock blasting through the speakers. He moved without thinking too hard, and let his subconscious take over. Soon Jax had the stove fired up with various sauces simmering as he prepped the veggies and finally, the beef tenderloin. It was so obvious that the perfect protein had escaped him at first, but it was Beth's favorite and a perfectly grilled tenderloin was always first class.

He moved back to the stove, tasting and seasoning the sauces he was working on. That would be the final decision. Would it be a red wine reduction or a classic peppercorn sauce? He couldn't decide. Jax tossed the spoon to the counter and focused instead on the garnish. The Springs and Stillwater restaurant was known for its fresh produce, sourced as locally as possible. Of course, that wasn't possible during the long winter months but now that the weather had started to warm up, more and more offerings were coming available and the promise of a summer full of fresh ingredients excited him.

If I'll be here. He'd forgotten all about the job applications he'd sent off a few weeks earlier. It actually amazed him that he hadn't given them any thought. Not since Bria.

Bria.

Of course, he'd been so busy and caught up in spending time with her, he hadn't had time to think of anything else. But he knew it wasn't just that he'd been busy. It was more than that, but he didn't want or have the time to think about it. Not yet.

Jax focused on the details in front of him. He sprinkled salt and pepper on the beef before laying it on the hot grill. It would take a careful watch to be sure he didn't overcook it, but when it came to steak, it was second nature to Jax. He whipped up a simple vinaigrette and piled a plate with fresh greens that had just come from the greenhouse, and topped it with pea shoots and a drizzle of the dressing. The steak only took a few more minutes, and by then his plate was ready with the garnish. All he needed was to decide on the sauce. The peppercorn was perfect. But it wasn't quite right...at the last minute, Jax chose the red wine reduction and carefully placing the tenderloin on top of the carefully prepared potato mash, he dressed it with just the right touch of sauce.

He finished with a garnish and stood back to admire his work.

It was beautiful and more than that, it looked delicious. Slade would love it. It wasn't too dainty and "fluffy" but it was definitely not boring and ordinary. It was perfect. He took his cellphone out and snapped a picture, texting it to Slade.

How about this for your special question?

To Jax's surprise, he hadn't even finished tidying up the

dishes, putting them in the industrial dishwasher, when his phone beeped a response.

Looks perfect. I'll be right down.

"Are you kidding?" Jax spoke aloud and laughed. He should have guessed his friend would be up in the middle of the night, too. He'd learned that rock stars didn't seem to sleep especially rock stars who had a big decision weighing on their minds.

Jax finished wiping down the counter, grabbed two sets of cutlery and waited for Slade, which didn't take long.

"It smells friggin' good in here." Slade, looking as if he'd slept in his clothes, slid into the kitchen and immediately grabbed a fork. "This looks amazing. Steak, huh?"

"Not just steak. Tenderloin. Every time I've ever made it for Beth, she's totally melted."

Slade narrowed his eyes. "What are you doing making my girl melt?"

"Not like that." Jax laughed and handed Slade the steak knife, although he questioned the safety in that decision. "Try it." He moved away to give Slade space to test the meal. "I thought you could start with some simple scallops, a nice glass of wine and then after, finish with a—"

Jax stopped talking when it was clear his friend hadn't heard a word he said. Slade's eyes were closed; his fork hovered in the air. For a moment, Jax considered taking a photo for bribery material later on, but decided against it. "It's good, right?" He crossed his arms over his chest, confident in his skills.

It was better than good, and they both knew it.

After a moment, Slade finished chewing the piece in his mouth. "Holy shit, Jax. This is perfect. Something about that sauce...and the beef...it's perfect. What were you saying about after?"

"Crème brûlée. It's simple and elegant, and I have the best

pastry chef in the Rockies. I'll have him make some up special."

Slade put down his fork and dropped his head into his hands. "Now I just have to figure everything else out."

"I thought you had the details all put together already." Jax seized the opportunity to take a bite of steak himself. The little picnic he'd shared with Bria hadn't done much to satisfy his hunger, especially considering all they'd really done was work up an appetite. "What else do you need?" He gestured to the meal.

Slade looked up at him with tired and very stressed eyes. "I need ambience. I need romance. I need a song, man. A song."

"A song?" That wasn't something that would have occurred to Jax, but then again, he hadn't much thought of proposals of any kind. A song made perfect sense for Slade, though. "Do you really think Beth needs all that? Won't she just be blown away with the whole proposal thing itself?"

Slade looked at him as if he'd lost his mind, but Jax was pretty sure it wasn't him who'd lost it.

"Look. I almost have the last verse worked out. That's the part that has me stuck. But I need a deadline to get it done."

"A deadline?"

"I work best under pressure."

Jax shrugged. "You just let me know what I can do to help. Besides cook, of course." He shrugged and took another bite of steak.

"Tonight." Slade jumped up and paced the kitchen. "I'm going to do it tonight. I want a private dining experience. We'll do it in my suite. I'll get a waitress from—"

"No."

"No, what?"

"Not in your suite." Jax smiled as it all came together in his mind. "I know the perfect place."

Chapter Ten

WHEN JAX ASKED Bria for a favor, of course she was going to say yes. It was Jax and if she was totally honest, she secretly hoped the favor was sexual in nature.

She hadn't expected to wear a waitress uniform in the middle of the mountains and help him set up a table and chairs at the very same natural springs she now kind of thought of as their private pool. She reached up to hang another lantern in a tree, but couldn't help let her gaze fall to the steaming water below where less than twenty-four hours earlier, she'd had her legs wrapped around Jax's hard, slippery body while he drove into her and made her scream out into the night air.

She stepped down off the stepladder and needing to look away, she turned and ran straight into that same hard body. This time dressed in his chef whites.

Jax's arms came around her to keep her close while his lips pressed a hard, hot kiss to her lips. "I know what you're thinking," he whispered gruffly in her ear.

"You have no idea."

"Oh yes." His hand slipped down her side to cup her ass. "I

know exactly what you're thinking." He squeezed and made his point before he kissed her again, this time with a hunger and promise for later.

She managed to pull out of his grasp, because if she didn't she would lose whatever self-control remained and they'd totally blow things for Slade. Bria forced herself to remain focused on the plan Jax had laid out for her. Slade was going to take Beth for a hike to the springs, where apparently they'd had a private moment, too. Bria tried not to let that bother her; she wanted to think of the remote pools as her private hideaway with Jax. But she wasn't naive enough to think that no one else had been up there before. Jax might have even taken other women there before.

No.

She would not let that thought enter her mind and spoil the memories of their night together. And what memories they were. The lingering heat of his fingers on her body would have made sleep all but impossible, if she hadn't been so worn out from being an impromptu labor and delivery coach. As it was, she'd been able to get a good rest and fend off her grandmother's questions the next morning. She wasn't quite sure how she'd accomplished the latter, but Mona had seemed a little tired, so besides a few questions about the baby, there hadn't been much more of an interrogation. To be honest, Bria was a little disappointed. She knew Mona liked Jax and her grandmother was pretty open-minded about a lot of things. No doubt, she'd be nothing but encouraging to any kind of relationship or hookup or whatever it was they were doing.

She glanced over her shoulder at Jax, who was back at his makeshift kitchen, which consisted of a portable grill and a hot plate set up behind a stand of trees. He was so focused as he worked on his food. It was sexy as hell to watch and more than a little distracting. The smell that came from his direction made her mouth water and combined with the very hot chef who prepared the delicious food, Bria had a very hard time focusing on the task.

But Slade would be there with Beth soon and she was not going to be the one responsible for screwing up the most romantic evening of Beth's life. Every woman deserved a proposal like the one Slade had planned and despite the fact that she'd been surprised Jax had asked her for help, she'd also been incredibly honored. They had a ton of friends who would've jumped at the chance. No doubt all of them were busy, but it didn't matter. She was happy to help. So she better get to it.

Bria went through the mental checklist. The table was set; lanterns were hung in the trees; she'd need to light the candles soon, but they could wait. She still needed—the guitar. She hustled down the trail and retrieved Slade's guitar from the front seat of the truck. She grabbed the lighter while she was there and after she propped the guitar up by a nearby tree, far enough from the water that it wouldn't accidentally get knocked in, she lit all the candles and stashed the stepladder back in the truck.

Just in time, too, because she heard the rustling in the trees and voices coming up the trail. She dashed over to the makeshift kitchen and Jax, to get ready.

"They're coming."

A strong arm wrapped around her waist, and Jax nuzzled into her neck. "With any luck, they won't be the only ones—"

"Stop it." She swatted him away, but her body was instantly on fire from his words and exactly what he would have said if she'd allowed him to finish his thoughts.

He laughed and pulled her back to him so her body was pressed up against the solid length of him. He smelled of onions and garlic and absolute deliciousness.

"Ssh." She turned her head and gave him a kiss before adding, "Let's watch."

Jax shrugged but together they watched as Slade led Beth into the clearing and she held her hand to her mouth as she took in the romantic setup. Slade led her to the table and held the chair out for her. That was Bria's cue. She tried to wiggle out of Jax's grasp, but he wouldn't let her go until he spun her around and kissed her thoroughly.

The kiss left her reeling and she watched dumbly as Jax returned to his cooktop with nothing more than a wink for her. The man did know how to affect her, but judging by the bulge in his chef pants, she clearly had a similar effect on him.

She straightened her blouse, slung the white napkin over her arm, grabbed the bottle of the wine and headed out to play her role.

THE ENTIRE NIGHT was incredibly romantic and Bria was totally swept up in it all. She played her role as the waitress perfectly, delivering the beautiful meal Jax prepared and then making herself scarce as quickly and quietly as possible, only appearing to clear the plates and pour more wine. She would have thought maybe she missed her true calling as a waitress, if it wasn't for the fact that she was wound up tighter than an elastic and she only had one table to worry about. The stress was killing her. But with the final delivery of the crème brûlée, the food portion of the evening was over.

"This is it," Jax whispered, the way they'd been whispering all night so as not to be overheard by the lovebirds. Their job was to deliver food and blend in to the background. "I'm going to take the rest of the food to the truck so we don't attract any animals."

"I think the only animal is right here." She couldn't resist the comment that only a few weeks ago would have been totally out of character for her. But with Jax, she didn't know what her character was anymore. He brought out the fun playfulness in her, and she liked it. A lot.

He grabbed her apron and pulled her toward him. "You know I'll be more than happy to show you exactly what kind of animal I can be." He kissed her, and she matched his heat with plenty of her own. "Later," he whispered and pulled away.

When he left with the cooler, Bria leaned back against the trunk of the tree and let out a long sigh, stopping just short of releasing a groan of frustration. It was neither the time nor the place to act on her increasing attraction for Jax. She assumed after they had sex, the flame would have been doused. Clearly she'd been wrong. Their night of intense lovemaking had only fueled the fire. Now that she knew just exactly how incredible the sex would be, she wanted more.

The strains of a guitar playing floated through the air, reminding Bria where she was, and why she was there. She turned to peek through the bushes. Slade had retrieved his guitar and was playing for Beth. It wasn't a song Bria was familiar with, and when she paid closer attention, she realized the lyrics were about them. Her heart clenched a little bit. It was the single most romantic thing she'd ever heard.

By instinct, Bria rummaged around under the prep table and found her camera. She was in the habit of traveling with it everywhere and it was never far away. She adjusted the settings and put it to her face, capturing the romantic moment from a variety of angles. Jealousy burned in her gut as she zoomed in on Slade. It was written all over his face how much he loved her. Would Bria ever see that? Would she ever be able to look at a man and see that much love in his eyes for her?

The questions that floated through her head took her off guard. She'd never wanted that for herself. She'd never pretended that type of love would ever be in her future. Not until Jax.

That was crazy. She tried to push the idea out of her head.

But she couldn't. Why would Jax have anything to do with such feelings? They were just fooling around. It didn't mean anything.

Did it?

Bria took pictures without even realizing what she was seeing. Her mind was so occupied with the crazy idea that she and Jax could have a relationship that it took her a moment to realize Slade had put the guitar down and had reached into his pocket. She swallowed the lump that had suddenly formed in her throat and zoomed in on Beth.

The sheer amount of candles she'd placed around the clearing lit up the couple and cast a soft glow on Beth's face as a tear slid down her cheek. When Slade pulled out a diamond ring, the large stone reflected the light and Bria adjusted her settings quickly and continued to click.

Part of her felt as if she intruded on such a private moment, but her instinct took over as she moved silently throughout the bushes in an effort to capture the happy couple from a different position. When Beth nodded and said yes, Bria made sure to capture the sheer happiness on her face and the subsequent joy from Slade as he jumped to his feet and pulled her into his arms. Their kiss was beautiful and so full of love, it radiated off them. It wasn't until they pulled apart, pressing their foreheads together in a moment so intimate and private, that Bria put the camera down. She'd captured that moment, too, but it no longer felt right to be part of things.

She tucked the camera back into her bag as Jax returned. "Hey," he whispered as he knelt next to her. "It looks like our job is over. I'll come back and clean up later. What do you say we get out of here?"

Bria turned so she looked up into his gorgeous face. She might never experience the romance and pure love that Slade and Beth so clearly shared, and whatever it was that was going on with Jax might only be temporary, but she sure as hell could enjoy every second of it. And that's exactly what she planned to do. She licked her lower lip, biting down just a little in the way she knew would drive him crazy.

"Sounds like a plan."

GETTING Bria back to his room was the only thing on Jax's mind as he navigated down the rough mountain road. Okay, it wasn't the only thing on his mind. In fact, the last time they'd been in his truck driving on that very same road was also forefront in his mind. But he needed to focus and he was done with quickies in the truck or sex under the stars. This time he wanted her on his bed, where he could take his time with her.

He was so busy trying to keep his desire in check, it took him a few minutes to realize she'd fallen silent. He glanced over. Bria stared out the window at the dark forest. "You okay?"

She nodded and turned toward him, but he couldn't quite make out the expression on her face in the dark. "I'm good. I was just thinking about how incredible tonight was. I can't believe all the time and—"

"It was impressive. Who would have thought Slade Black could be so romantic?" He tried to laugh off the serious atmosphere in the truck, and Bria joined in, but he could tell her heart wasn't in it. "Women like that romance stuff, huh?"

"Yes. I mean…most do."

"Not you?"

She shook her head. "No. I've never been much of a softie like that. I don't need all that relationship stuff."

"Relationship stuff? Or romance stuff?" The idea that Bria was a loner like himself disturbed him, and he couldn't quite figure out why. Maybe it was because from the moment he'd met her, he'd somehow stopped thinking of himself as a loner

And the more time he spent with her, the more time he felt as though he might be coupled up. And stranger still, instead of freaking him out, he kind of liked it. All of which was ridiculous, anyway, considering they hadn't even known each other a month.

"Aren't they the same thing?"

"Not at all." She turned to face him, the smile that he'd grown to love lighting up her face once again. "You can be romantic without a relationship."

"But wouldn't someone be more inclined to be romantic to someone they were in a relationship with?"

She shrugged. "Honestly, I wouldn't know either way."

The thought that Bria had never experienced a romantic moment or a relationship stopped him. More than that, the desire to give her both surprised him with its intensity. He had no business saying anything, or making a promise he certainly couldn't keep, but it didn't stop him from asking, "What would you say about it?"

"About what? Romance? Or a relationship?"

"Either."

She didn't answer right away but after a moment, she squeezed her eyes shut for just a fraction of a second, as if she might actually be considering what he was really asking. Her lips parted but no sound came out and she closed them again.

"Well?"

"I'm not sure what you're asking."

He pulled into the staff parking, took the truck out of gear and faced her. "I think you know exactly what I'm asking." The truth was Jax didn't really know what he was asking himself. There was no way he was in any position to ask her for a relationship. He didn't do relationships. He did leaving. Moving on. New places, new faces. That was the exact opposite of relationships. But he couldn't tear his eyes away from Bria and the way she watched him, as if he might just be promising her something she would actually reach out and grab on to.

"I think I'd say.. " She licked her lips in that way that made him want to kiss her breathless before she continued. "Okay."

"Okay?" He'd been expecting something a bit grander. A bit more monumental.

Bria threw her head back and laughed, the sound coming from somewhere deep inside her. "Okay." She looked up again and brushed her long, dark hair from her face. "Romance? Relationship? I've never had either one, and I've always said that I'd try anything once, so why not?"

Jax didn't know what he could offer her and he wasn't a total idiot. Even if that's exactly how she made him feel whenever she was near, never mind the way his brain totally left his body when she kissed him, touched him and ran her hands down—it didn't matter. What mattered was that Bria had never had romance, and dammit if that wasn't one thing he *could* give her.

Without saying another word, he slipped from the truck and as quickly as possible, darted to her door, which he opened with a flourish that he knew was ridiculous. She giggled, but the laughter died on her lips as he reached in and scooped her up in his arms.

"Jax."

He kicked the truck door behind him and walked with her cradled in his arms, toward the door to the staff apartments.

"Jax."

She wriggled in his grip, so he pulled her into his chest and squeezed her ass for good measure. "Settle down, or I'm going to drop you."

"You're going to drop me anyway. You're crazy. I'm too heavy. Put me down. You're going to—"

He silenced her with a deep kiss. When he pulled up,

leaving her lips swollen, her eyes closed, he said, "You are as light as one of my infamous soufflés and when I put you down next, it will be in my bed where I don't plan on letting you up for the rest of the night."

"You're crazy."

"Maybe I am."

SHE DIDN'T WANT to let herself believe it was anything more than sex. She couldn't let herself believe it was more than that. But the way he looked at her when he talked about romance and relationships... Did that mean he wanted one? And if he did...did she? She'd never had either, it was true.

Romance—well, that was just due to the men she'd dated.

Relationships, that was her. And maybe it had something to do with the men she'd dated, too. But either way, Bria had never considered the lack of either one of those things a problem that needed solving. Until that moment.

With Jax's strong arms wrapped around her, carrying her up the stairs of the apartment building as if she weighed nothing, her thoughts went a million different places all at the same time. She couldn't formulate a cohesive thought. And the craziest part of it was, she didn't care. All that mattered was Jax's hard chest pressing against her, the way he looked at her with so much desire in his eyes, and the fact that they were headed to his bed. The only place she wanted to be.

It took forever to get up the stairs and down the hall to his apartment, but finally, after what seemed like forever, he shifted her in his arms to jostle the key in the lock.

"Jax, you can put me down."

"Not until you're in my bed." His voice was gruff and full of need. It sent a spark of lust directly to her core and she closed her mouth against any further protest.

He managed the lock and they stepped inside before he kicked the door shut behind him with such power that the picture on the wall shook, but Bria hardly paid it any mind as Jax made a beeline to his bedroom, where he deposited her on the bed with more care than she'd expected. She'd expected a ferocious need, a ripping of clothes, a need to be naked and flesh to flesh with him. Instead, he stood over her, assessed her body with his eyes, and took in every inch of her before he finally spoke.

"Don't move."

Jax turned and left the room before she could protest that she indeed wanted to move—all over his body until he was inside her and filled every inch of her.

Bria dropped back against the comforter on his bed and breathed in the scent of him. The moonlight outside lit up the space just enough so that she could see the bed she laid on was neatly made and there were no clothes or any other form of mess on the floor. She lifted her head up to take in the rest of the space. The entire room was tidy. Besides a dresser with a bottle of cologne and a few papers, nothing marked the space. There were no personal pictures or any of the usual signs of a bachelor she would have expected from a single guy. In fact, there was nothing much at all.

She didn't have time to think about it because Jax was back with a tray full of items. He didn't say a word as he moved around the room and lit candles until the room was lit in a sexy glow. It reminded Bria of the romantic scene they'd just left behind in the woods, only there was something more sensual about the candles in the bedroom. Romantic, yes. But sexy, no doubt.

"Nice touch." She leaned back on her arms, pushed her chest up and stretched her legs out in front of her.

"You like it?" Jax didn't wait for an answer, but moved back to the tray and deftly opened the bottle of white wine to pour two glasses. He handed her one, but before he joined her on the bed, he grabbed a remote she hadn't noticed and pressed a button.

Music she didn't recognize floated from speakers she hadn't seen in the shadows of the room, and then and only then did he crawl on to the bed to join her.

"I know it's not a gourmet candlelit dinner in the woods, but—"

"It's perfect." Bria's eyes filled with tears, which was ridiculous because there was nothing more to it. What she had going on with Jax—it was nothing. Just a fling and even if it was more—it wasn't. It was stupid to even think about it.

"Bria." Jax's fingers lifted her chin so she looked at him. She hadn't even realized she'd looked away. "What's going on? What's wrong?"

"Nothing's wrong." God, why did she have to be such a girl? It was ridiculous. "Honestly. I think I'm just tired."

He looked at her for a moment. Really looked at her, as if he looked for something more. She had nothing more to give. Finally, he smiled. "I hope you're not too tired." He took the wine glass from her hand and put both glasses on the nightstand before he straddled her body with his own. "Because I've got plans for you tonight. And they don't involve sleeping."

If his plans for her were anything like what she'd been going over in her mind for the last few days, Bria would be more than happy to give up sleep for the sake of Jax's hands on her skin, his lips on hers, and his body inside her. Hell, she'd be happy to never sleep again if that was on the table.

"Stand up." His voice was quiet but strong. There was no denying his request. Not that Bria would have. There was something about the way Jax could take command and leave her feeling totally in control at the same time that made her hotter than she thought possible.

She slid to the edge of the bed until she could dangle her

feet over and place them on the floor. She stood slowly, until she stood only inches from him. The heat coming off his body radiated directly to her skin, even through the layers of clothing between them. Yet, despite the heat and the moisture that pooled between her legs, a shiver ran through her.

Jax twitched his lips up in response. "Do I make you nervous?"

"Not even a little bit," she lied easily. The truth was he made her very nervous. The strength of her body's sharp and almost desperate reaction to him terrified her.

He reached out and trailed his fingers down her neck, to where her blouse was held closed. She closed her eyes against his intense gaze. A sigh escaped her lips as his tender touch reached the first button. Instead of the violent destruction of her clothing from the other night, he took his time, worked each button through its hole. His moves were painfully slow and deliberate. If he was trying to drive her crazy, it was working. With each button he freed, her arousal only intensified until she was positive she'd burst into flames if he didn't touch her.

"Bria," Jax said, his voice full of barely constrained passion of his own. "Look at me."

She did, because there was no way she couldn't. His eyes were dark with need, his own breath coming fast to match the heaving of her chest.

He pulled the fabric of her top to the side, exposing her lacy bra, and spanned his hands over her waist. "You are incredible."

Her breath hitched at his words. Never before had she been with a man who spoke to her with such passion and genuine heat in his words, while his hands were…oh, God, his hands.

Jax moved his hands up her torso until he pushed her blouse from her shoulders; it puddled at her feet. Bria tipped her head back and tried without success to calm her breathing as he focused his attention on her breasts, cupping each one gently as if they would shatter in his grasp.

She was about to shatter in his grasp.

"Jax, I—"

Her words disappeared as his mouth met hers, kissing her long and deep until her knees were weak. When he'd had his fill, he freed her from her pants, so she stood in her bra and panties before him. Normally she'd feel exposed and vulnerable, but the way Jax looked at her, with hunger in his eyes, Bria felt powerful. "Your turn. I want to see you."

And she did. She wanted nothing more than to lay her eyes on his body while he looked at her that way. And she wasn't going to wait any longer. Bria reached for him, undoing the buttons of his chef jacket. She tried to move as slowly as he'd done, but she was out of patience. Soon, she'd divested him of his jacket and pants. He reached down and tugged his white t-shirt over his head, leaving her to stare at the rock-hard chest in front of her. Sure, she'd seen him in the water the night before, and she obviously had some idea of what was under those clothes, but to see his hard muscles, his skin glinting in the candlelight, only inches in front of her was a completely different story. He bent and slipped his shorts down over his legs. Bria took her time to take in everything before her. She already knew what he had. She'd become well acquainted with every part of him, but somehow this, letting her eyes wander over every inch of gorgeous manliness, was different. More intimate.

She swallowed hard. "*You* are incredible."

He smiled, and gestured toward her own undergarments. As slowly as she could and with as much sexiness as she could muster, Bria reached around her back, and unclasped her bra before she slid her panties down her legs. Exposed, she stood in front of him and let him take his own appraisal.

By the look in his eyes, he more than liked what he saw.

And when he pulled her to him so their bodies were pressed up together and took her mouth in another hard, deep kiss, Bria felt herself come completely undone. Never before had she allowed herself to be so open, so honest with a man. The idea of exposing herself to Jax in such a raw way scared her beyond comprehension, but also, she couldn't imagine any other way for them to come together.

He backed her up until her legs hit the back of the bed and then eased her down to the mattress, never breaking the kiss. As if she weighed nothing, he lifted her and slid her back before leaving her mouth to kiss a trail down her entire body. With every kiss he left on her skin, her body buzzed a little more until finally she thought she would combust. "Jax." Her voice came out rough with desire. "I need you." He stopped in his treatment of her body and looked up at her. "Now."

He didn't need any more invitation than that. He only took a second to grab a condom from the nightstand before he sheathed himself and then he hovered over her body, his arms bracing him on either side of her head. "You have no idea how much I need you, Bria."

For half a second, she wondered whether there was more behind his words than he was saying. How did he need her? More than what they had? But all thought vanished from her brain as he slid inside her, filling her with that need. She looked directly into his eyes, met him thrust for thrust, until the only thing either of them needed was each other.

Chapter Eleven

IT HAD BEEN ALMOST a week since the big Slade and Beth engagement and everyone at the Springs was buzzing about it. Everyone who knew, that was. The happy couple had asked all their friends to keep it quiet for the time being. They wanted to enjoy their happy news without having to field a million questions from the press; being in the public eye the way they were, they knew it was inevitable, but their friends were happy to give them as much time alone as they could. Even if it was only a few days.

Mona was beside herself when Bria told her the happy news. She wanted every detail and was more than a little put out that her granddaughter hadn't told her about it or her special role in the night, earlier.

"I don't know how many times I have to tell you the same story, Grandma. If I didn't know better, I'd think you were starting to go senile." Bria laughed as Mona threw a cushion at her head.

"I keep asking you because I'm trying to make you feel bad for not telling me beforehand."

Bria sighed and shook her head. It wasn't the first time

she'd heard the argument. "I had to keep quiet, Grandma. I told you, they made me swear not to say anything until it was over." That wasn't entirely true; in fact, Jax and Slade had said nothing of the sort, but Bria knew her grandmother too well and she knew Mona would never have been able to keep such an exciting thing a secret.

"Surely Simon wouldn't have…oh well." Mona waved her hand. "It's over now. But don't think I'm going to forget about it, missy—you owe me big time. But for now, tell me everything. Every little detail. Again."

Bria sighed, but she didn't really mind. Even if she had already told Mona everything about the proposal. Multiple times. Well, not everything. She did leave out the part about her and Jax after they left, but technically, that really didn't have anything to do with the actual event. She also didn't mention the photos she took. It would have been easy to just show Mona the pictures instead of trying to recreate everything again with her retelling. But for some reason, Bria kept quiet about them.

When she was done telling Mona, again, Bria pushed herself up from the couch and stretched her arms up over her head, arching her back to work out the kinks. Her body was still a little sore from the workout she'd had with Jax. But it was a good sore, and it was starting to fade. He'd been so busy over the last week, they'd hardly had time for more than a few stolen kisses here and there. It was better than nothing, and considering she wasn't ready to admit their relationship—or whatever it was—to her grandmother or anyone else, she'd have to be satisfied with what she could get.

It was obvious her secrecy bothered Jax. He didn't say anything, but she saw the way he looked at her, when she jerked back to put space between them if she thought someone was coming, or how she pretended she barely even knew him when her grandmother was around. It was ridiculous, too, because Mona knew they'd been spending time together to take the photos. And even if she didn't know that, Mona wasn't stupid.

"Well, if you're not going to tell me any more than that, I think I'll go find Simon and Beth and get the details myself." Mona got to her feet and Bria couldn't help but notice she moved a little slower than usual.

"Are you okay, Grandma? Did you take your pills today?"

"I'm fine." She brushed Bria off. "The hot water makes me feel like I'm twenty again. Okay, maybe thirty. But it makes me feel damn good and for this body to feel damn good, that's saying something. I should probably get down to the pools today. It's been awhile is all."

"You look—"

"I don't look any way," Mona snapped. She caught herself and her voice softened as she changed the subject. "What do you have planned today?"

Bria could have pushed the matter but there was no point. And if she made her grandma mad and put her on the defensive, it would only cause more problems. With a sigh, she let it go.

"I'm going to head down to town and get some more pictures developed. Carmen and Dylan agreed to look at them again now that things have calmed down a bit." As much as things could calm down with a newborn in the house, Bria thought. But it was a better offer than none and considering she still had to give Kristie a call—something she'd been putting off for days—she'd take what she could get as far as Carmen and Dylan were concerned.

Mona didn't seem to hear her, or if she had, she didn't seem to think the fact that her granddaughter's career hung in the balance of a couple of brand-new, over-stressed parents running on very little sleep, important. "That's nice. Is Jax taking you to town?"

The question caught her off guard and she stumbled over her response. A fact her grandma actually did seem to pick up on. Mona's unpredictability was beginning to annoy her.

"He is." Bria finally spat out an answer to what was a very simple question. "He has a few things to do and has to talk to a friend about some meat or something, so he said it would be no big deal."

"I'm sure it won't." Mona wiggled her eyebrows and laughed heartily.

"Grandma "

"I may be old, kiddo, but I'm not a nun."

"Grandma "

Mona only laughed harder. "I'm also not blind, sweetheart. I see the way you look at him."

"I don't—"

"And the way he looks at you."

With that, Bria looked away because she knew her reaction would show all over her face. How did Jax look at her? She thought she knew. She thought he looked at her like a man who was, if not in love, in serious like. And she liked him too. A lot. More than she wanted to admit to anyone. Especially him. Because what if he didn't feel the same way? What if she exposed herself to something that he didn't feel and what if…it didn't matter. The whole thing was still too new for it to be anything more than it was anyway. Relationships or whatever simply didn't happen that fast.

"Bria?"

She turned to see her grandma, the laughter gone from her face, looking more than a little concerned. "Do you want to tell me what's going on with Jax?"

Bria nodded and shook her head at the same time "There's nothing going on."

Mona looked as though she was going to argue the point. Instead, she smiled and winked. "Okay." Bria was about to leave so she could grab her camera bag when Mona's voice stopped her. "You know, I once gave Simon some advice about Beth. Do you know that he never thought it would work between them? After all, he's a musician and she's a single mom from a small town. How different can you get?"

Bria nodded. "And what did you tell him that changed everything?"

"It's simple, really. I told him that sometimes you need to take a good solid look at what it is you think you want and what it is that you need. And then you need to get out of your own damn way. And I think that advice applies equally to you, my dear."

Bria lifted an eyebrow in response.

"He took my advice and they were able to make it work because sometimes love, even when it doesn't make any sense, is more important than all the reasons not to love. When you need someone, your heart doesn't understand excuses. It only understands the need."

Bria sucked in a sharp breath. Need. Jax had said he needed her. Hell, she'd said that. But it was in bed, and it was…it wasn't the same thing. Was it?

It wasn't a question she could answer. And it certainly wasn't a question she could ask her grandma about. "I should go," she said instead. "Are you going to be okay, Grandma? Did you want me to get you a pill?"

"Go. Enjoy your afternoon with Jax." Mona waved her away with a wicked little grin. "I'll see you later."

IT TOOK ALL of Jax's willpower not to pull the truck off into the little back road he'd come to think of as *their* road and have his way with Bria. She looked downright delicious next to him in the truck and the need to be with her was ridiculously strong. She was a little drug that he could not get enough of, and the last week had given them no time to be together. He had two new cooks to train on the line. One of whom proved to be quite talented, the other one…well, he'd need more work.

Between training them and catering for a few special events as well as the regular dinner services, Jax had been worn out. He'd done his best to seek out Bria for some private moments, but there'd been no time to be alone together. Not unless he felt like sneaking around like a teenager after curfew. And he wasn't in a hurry to do that, mostly because he'd passed out from exhaustion the moment he got back to his apartment, but also because he was tired of keeping whatever it was that was going on between them a secret. Bria didn't seem to be in any hurry to tell her grandma about them and whenever she pulled away and put distance between them as if she'd been caught with her hand in the cookie jar, it stung.

More than he cared to admit.

Hell, he didn't know what was happening between them any more than she probably did, but what he did know was that he wanted to be with her in whatever capacity that looked like for the moment. He'd figure out *later* when he had to.

"Why don't you slide over here?"

Bria turned and her dark hair slid across her shoulders. "Were you looking for another—"

"No." He cut her off quickly before the idea could take root in his mind. Too late. From the tightening of his jeans, the idea had already made an impact. "But I was hoping for a kiss."

She smiled. Damn, he loved that smile. When she let down her wall long enough to just be open and real, her beauty took his breath away. As cliché as it sounded, even to his own jaded ears, it was true. And it didn't surprise anyone more than him how okay with it he really was.

Bria unclipped her seatbelt and slid across the bench until she was snuggled up under his arm. He pulled her close, enjoying the feel of her slight body against his. It felt right. Really right.

"How long do you need to be in town?" she asked. "I don't want to keep you. I know how busy you've been."

"I'm good. I'll drop you at the shop and then I'll be over at the Grizzly Paw talking to Archer. So whenever you're done, just come and find me and we can go. Take as long as you need."

"Sounds good to me."

"You know what sounds really good to me?" He navigated the truck down to the main street, wishing they were back on the mountain road, so he'd have even longer to be with her.

"What's that?" Her voice was light, full of teasing.

He pulled up in front of the general store and looked over to see Cynthia in the front window, adjusting the new display with gardening tools and seed packets. "I guess you'll have to wait until later to find out."

Bria shook her head and was about to slide away from him and out the door when he grabbed her hand and pulled her back to him. He should have cared that Cynthia could probably see them, and would either be jealous or tell everyone in town what she saw, or both, but he didn't. All he cared about was Bria's lips on his.

He kissed her thoroughly before he released her. "I'll see you later."

"Oh yes you will." Her words were full of promise, and as he watched her make her way across the sidewalk and into the store, Jax knew it was a promise he was looking forward to having fulfilled.

"TELL me you have some venison for me." Jax slid onto the bar stool across from Archer.

"Hey to you, too." Archer automatically poured them each a beer from the tap. "And no, I don't." He set the beer in front of Jax.

"You better be kidding." Jax had been afraid of exactly what Archer was telling him, but he wasn't totally surprised. The truth was, he hadn't given the menu for the critic the thought it deserved, especially considering it was a career-defining moment. And by putting the pressure on Archer to deliver him fresh venison, Jax knew he was passing the buck, never mind the pun, directly to his buddy.

"Sorry, man. I haven't had a chance to get out in the bush and I know you don't want any of last year's—"

"No." If he was going to use it, it had to be fresh. Or at least, fresher than twelve months of sitting in a freezer. "I'll think of something else."

"Trust me, no one is more sorry than I am." Archer pulled a stool over and sat across from Jax. "I want out of this place and into the bush more than you know. I'm going a little crazy around here."

"So go." Samantha, the owner of the Grizzly Paw and Archer's best friend, came out from the kitchen just in time to hear his complaining. "No one is keeping you here."

Archer rolled his eyes at Jax, who had to do a double take at Samantha. She was normally so easygoing, but something was clearly bothering her. Sam kicked a box and slammed her fist down on the bar. Oh yes, something was really bothering Sam.

"I never said I was going anywhere, Sam." Archer held his hands up in defense. "I was just saying—"

"I know what you were saying. And especially what you weren't saying." She put her hands on her hips, an action that had Jax ready to retreat. He'd never seen Sam fired up like this, and he thought he liked it a whole lot better that way.

"I really wasn't saying anything." Archer was exceedingly calm, and Jax was suitably impressed. "Whatever is going on with you, it's not my fight. Maybe you should talk to Trent about—"

"There is nothing going on with me. That's the problem. And if I have to talk to Trent about it, then that totally defeats the purpose."

"The purpose of what?"

Jax sat back and kept quiet. He'd been around enough angry females to know when it was safer just to keep his mouth shut.

"Never mind. I'm going out."

Sam grabbed her purse and headed through the bar, leaving the men staring after her before either of them knew exactly what had happened.

Archer shook his head and lifted his beer to his mouth.

"What was that all about?" Jax laughed and drank his beer.

"That was an issue for Trent to deal with. His woman, his problem. And if I'm right, she's all wound up because of him."

"What did Trent do?"

"It's what he didn't do," Archer said. "Sam's watching all her friends have babies, get engaged and she's just…"

"Ahh." Jax shook his head. "Just another reason to stay single, right?" He asked the question mostly out of reflex because it was what Archer and Jax did. As pretty much the only single men in their group of friends, it was easier to laugh off the trouble of their coupled-up comrades. And usually, Jax meant it. But as he laughed along with Archer, for the first time, his heart wasn't into it. Instead, thoughts of Bria popped up, which was ridiculous because he'd never in his life wanted to be coupled up or tied down or in any way committed to a woman beyond one night. But Bria changed that. Or was changing that. The laughter died on his lips.

"What's up with you, Jax?" Archer filled his beer again. "Seems like you have something on your mind, too. Everyone around here is losing it. Maybe it's the whole spring fever thing."

"I'm not losing anything." Jax stood up and stretched. "I'm just starting to wonder about things."

"Not you too. I heard a rumor you were spending a lot of time with a pretty brunette."

That got Jax's attention. "Where did you hear that?" Not that he cared if someone thought he'd hooked up with Bria. Not really. It was true, anyway, but he was fairly sure Bria wouldn't like it. And wasn't that what was bothering him? Archer went to wait on a customer who'd come in and taken a booth in the far end of the pub, and Jax used the time to try to pull his thoughts together. He liked being with Bria. A lot. Probably too much. But she'd made it clear it was temporary. And that'd been fine with him. Except, when he thought about never seeing her again, never feeling her body move under his, never listening to the way she got spooled up and excited when she started talking about photography, he couldn't imagine it. What was even more telling was, he was no longer sure he wanted to imagine it.

His hand went to his breast pocket where he'd tucked away the unopened letter. It had been slid under his door and he'd found it right before going to meet Bria. If the letter had come a month ago, he would have ripped it open and would probably already be packing his bags. But that was a month ago, and a lot could change in such a short period. He hadn't ripped it open. He didn't know what it said. Hell, maybe they'd taken one look at his qualifications and denied him the job. But he knew that wasn't true. He'd never been turned down for a culinary position and with his resume only becoming more impressive, he knew that Angles had sent him an offer of employment. Taking the job would mean a lot of things. Depending on the start date, which, if he remembered correctly from the job posting, was in the next week or two, it might even mean he'd miss out on the visit from the critic, but he'd get a big salary increase, and even bigger increase in reputation and prestige. It was a fantastic opportunity. But along with those things, it would also mean leaving Cedar Springs and his growing group of friends. People he'd started to think of as family. People who were all coming through the door of the Grizzly Paw.

Jax turned his head at the commotion as Rhys and Kari came in, held the door for Carmen and finally Dylan, who was loaded down with a baby carrier, a diaper bag, and other various things slung over his shoulder. Jax rushed to help his friend, and caught sight of Trent and Samantha in a heated discussion on the sidewalk across the street.

"Best to leave them alone," Dylan said, seeing where Jax looked. "I wouldn't go near that drama if you paid me."

Jax laughed and joined everyone inside. No. He didn't need Trent and Sam's drama. He had plenty of his own to keep him busy and with the business of his friends and the excitement of the new baby, he'd have lots to keep his mind off the real reason he hadn't opened the envelope yet. Bria.

SHE FLIPPED THROUGH THE PICTURES, a smile on her face. It was the second batch of shots she'd printed off for Carmen and Dylan and they were good. Better than good. Bria knew they'd have to agree to let her use the shots for the magazine. How could they not? They were fantastic. She'd gone to the bakery across the street to view the pictures again because not only did Dream Puffs have the best cinnamon buns she'd ever tasted, but it also put distance between her and Cynthia.

Bria was positive Cynthia had feelings for Jax despite what he'd told her about it just being a fling. It might not have meant anything to Jax, but judging by the way Cynthia glared at Bria, there was definitely more to it, at least as far as she was concerned, and Bria didn't need that type of drama in her life. No thanks.

She continued to look through the pictures, eager to meet up with Jax at the Grizzly Paw. She moved quickly through the images when one stopped her. The natural springs reflected the water; the glow of the candles created an ethereal glow on the couple in the image. Slade and Beth. Their engagement. Of course. She'd totally forgotten that she'd put those images on the memory stick. Bria glanced through the shots, which had turned out beautifully.

She wasn't sure what she planned to do with the pictures and really, at the time she'd only picked up her camera as a reflex, not really planning anything in particular. But they weren't her images to do anything with. They were private and intimate shots of a special moment. Maybe she'd talk to Beth about them and give them to her to do what she wanted with. Bria shouldn't even have had them printed. Hopefully Cynthia hadn't paid any attention to what she was printing.

Bria stuffed the engagement shots in a separate envelope and put them in the back of her camera bag. The rest of the pictures she packed up, ready to show Carmen and Dylan and with one more bite of her cinnamon bun, she waved to Suzy and headed out onto the street.

There was something about spring in the mountains that Bria loved. Everything smelled crisp and clean, and everywhere she looked, trees and plants were coming to life. Every day there was more and more greenery and the sun felt a bit warmer, with the promise of summer right around the corner.

Bria found herself wondering what it would be like to spend summer in the mountains: sitting outside at the hot springs, letting the sun warm her face, making love to Jax on a warm summer night.

The thought hit her hard and knocked her a bit off guard, but instead of immediately squashing the thought, she let the idea roll around in her brain for a while, taking shape. She was so caught up in her own daydream it took her awhile to realize the ringing noise she heard was her cell phone.

Before it went to voicemail, Bria dug the phone out and seeing it was Kristie, pushed the button to answer the call.

"Hey, I've been meaning to call you." It was a lie and they both knew it. Bria had been avoiding Kristie, not wanting to tell her that most of her photographs had been given the kibosh. Plus, she still needed the official go-ahead from Carmen and the Harrison brothers before she could give Kristie any pictures at all to run.

"Like hell you've been meaning to call." Kristie didn't bother pussyfooting around the issue, but then again, she rarely did. "You've been avoiding me, Sheridan, and we both know it." It was never good when she called her by her last name. They were clearly in the business zone at the moment.

"I have pictures for you and you're going to love them."

"I better because I go to print tomorrow and if I don't get something to run, it won't just be your job on the chopping block here. I'm counting on you, Bria. Really."

"I know. And I promise, they're great pictures." She didn't bother mentioning that she didn't quite have the release signed yet. She'd need express permission before she could send the pictures anywhere. But she'd have it. Probably. There was no point stressing Kristie out further than she already had. "I've actually decided to take a whole new approach to this project." Bria braced herself for the response. To her surprise, Kristie didn't yell or freak out but simply sighed.

"A new approach? Bria, don't do this to me."

"You'll love it, I promise." Maybe Kristie wouldn't notice that the shots she included didn't actually give anything away as far as the Springs were concerned. And although they were definitely a more in-depth look at the resort than anyone else had had before, they still weren't the "behind closed doors" pictorial spread she knew her editor was looking for.

"I need you to deliver on your promise, Bria. And you know I hate giving ultimatums, but—"

"You will." Bria rolled her eyes. She was really sick of having her job held over her head at every turn. Maybe it wasn't worth it anymore. Freelancing started to look better and better and for the life of her, Bria couldn't remember why she'd been trying so hard to hang onto the staff position anyway. "It's okay, Kristie. I know you've been doing me a favor trying to keep this alive for me, but don't worry about it."

"What do you mean?"

Bria could hardly believe she'd said it too, but now that the words were out of her mouth, she meant them.

"I'm resigning my staff position. Effective immediately. And you know I'll make sure this project comes in for you. I don't want you losing your job, too."

Kristie let out another long sigh. "Bria, are you sure?"

She nodded even though her friend couldn't see her. "Yes. ' She didn't know exactly what she'd do, but she'd find something and freelancing wasn't so bad anyway. Especially if it gave her the freedom to stay in Cedar Springs a little bit longer. Because even though she was fighting it, there was something going on with Jax, and she definitely wanted the time to explore it, whatever *it* was.

Chapter Twelve

BRIA HAD RELUCTANTLY LEFT Jax outside the Stillwater. They'd had a great time in town and after she'd hung up with Kristie, she'd felt a weight lift off her, which allowed her to enjoy the afternoon with Jax's friends. It was nice to see Carmen again, in a less stressful situation and while their newborn had been passed around for snuggles by all the women in the room—except Bria—Carmen and Dylan signed the papers to release the images for use in the magazine.

Bria'd caught Jax watching her across the table. He looked happy but something else was going on behind those eyes, too. She made a mental note to ask him about it later, but once they were back in the truck, she'd totally forgotten about the moment and instead she listened while he chatted on about everyone they'd just left and filled Bria in on all the stories of his friends. By the time they got back up the mountain to the Springs, she felt as if she knew them all a little better, and a little part of her hoped to be one of those stories of coupledom one day too.

It was crazy, especially to Bria, that she'd even think like that after such a short time with Jax. She'd never even wanted a relationship before, let alone one that involved settling down in a small town where everyone knew your business. She could have laughed at the insanity of the situation, if it wasn't so real. It would seem even more real if she had time to talk to Jax about things to see whether he was on the same page as her. And it was a conversation she definitely wanted to have. Now that she'd quit her job, she was feeling reckless and there didn't seem to be a better time than the present.

Except there would have to be a better time because Jax had to get back to work. He'd said something about a busy dinner service and new guys he had to train and as much as he'd like to have dinner with her, he couldn't.

It was fine. She'd talk to him later. There would be plenty of time. Besides that, she'd promised her grandma they'd have dinner together. After all, she was supposed to be spending time with Mona, and she'd been so caught up in everything else, she'd neglected Mona.

"Grandma." Bria dropped her camera bag on her bed and knocked on the door to her grandma's adjoining suite before she walked in. "Are you back? We should go get a table. Jax promised to make your favorite tonight." Just saying his name made her flush, which was beyond ridiculous.

She walked through the living room, expecting to see Mona in the comfortable chair by the window with her knitting. The room was empty and a quick search of the bedroom and bathroom also turned up empty.

It had been hours since her grandma said she was going to soak in the pools; there was no way she could still be there. But with nowhere else to look, Bria headed back down the elevators to the pools. She'd only been in the pool room one time before, so she left her shoes at the door, exchanged them for the complimentary disposable flip-flops and after a quick check at the desk, confirmed what pool her grandmother should be in. She made her way through the large room, with a big public pool on one side, and the more private pools that had to be reserved to ensure privacy on the other. Mona was in pool six, so Bria made her way carefully along the slippery slate floor, looking for the tile peeking out of the foliage that held the number six.

She moved quietly up the path, into the private pool area, so she wouldn't startle her grandma. As soon as the pool came into view, she spoke quietly. "Grandma? Are you in here?"

There was no answer, so Bria moved all the way in and found Mona curled up in her robe on the chaise lounge next to the pool. "Grandma!" She ran quickly to her side and dropped to her knees next to the still figure. "Grandma. Wake up." She shook her arm and Mona's eyes flew open.

"Good grief, child. What are you doing? Trying to scare me into an early grave?"

"What?" Bria rocked back on her heels. "Trying to scare you? Are you kidding me? I thought you were…"

"Dead?" Mona struggled up to a sitting position. "Just because a lady my age is indulging in a mid-day nap does not mean she's dead."

"No. I—"

"You did too," Mona chastised. "The warm water made me tired, so I simply closed my eyes. I'm allowed to have a nap, am I not?"

"Yes. Of course." Bria felt a little dumber with every moment that passed. "I just…I'm sorry. I was worried."

Mona patted her hand and smiled. "No need to worry, my dear. I'm a tough old broad and I assure you that I'll give you plenty of notice before I decide to check out."

Bria laughed and stood before she dragged another chair over so she could sit down. "Are you getting hungry? Jax promised to cook your favorite lobster bisque if we made it down to the dining room tonight."

"He did, did he?" Mona wiggled her eyebrows. "I thought you said it wasn't like that with him."

"What?" Bria's hand flew to her chest. "Just because he promised to make you soup doesn't mean that there's anything between us."

"But there is?"

Bria didn't bother to deny it. "Let's go." She stood, extended a hand to her grandma and didn't miss the pain in Mona's eyes as she got to her feet and wrapped her robe tighter. "Grandma, I know you don't want to but I really think you need to take your pills."

Mona brushed her off. "The waters are—"

"I know the water is healing. But don't you think it would be extra healing if you used the therapy of the water combined with your medicine? I mean, it could only be a win."

Bria no longer bothered to dispute the healing powers of the natural hot springs. Since she'd been in those waters with Jax, there had been a whole lot of healing taking place, and maybe not in quite the way it was intended, but there'd been healing all right, there was no doubt about that.

"We'll talk about it later." Mona once again dismissed Bria's concerns. "Right now I'm hungry. And I think it's long overdue that you told me about Jax and what exactly is going on between the two of you."

IT WAS the first time in a long time that Jax worked the dinner service with a smile on his face the entire time. Perhaps it had something to do with the dark-haired beauty in the dining room. He'd gone to say hi and then of course personally served Bria and Mona their meals, and every time he saw her, she gave him a special smile or a wink, or even a little glance that told him in no uncertain terms that she wanted to get him alone almost as badly as he wanted to be alone with her. And he would be, too. Nothing was going to keep him away from her tonight.

He finished up the dinner rush and left the kitchen in the somewhat capable hands of his new hires, and the much more capable hands of his sous chef, Brent. He hung up his apron and went out to the dining room to join the women with a special dessert for them to share.

"How was dinner, ladies?" He slid into the booth next to Bria without waiting for an invitation and ignored Mona's raised eyebrow. Surely her granddaughter had told her something about the two of them. And wouldn't that be interesting to hear? More than a little, Jax wanted to know what Bria's take on everything was. And he'd hoped she might tell him directly instead of him having to guess or ask her outright. It would be really helpful information, especially in light of what this letter from Angles in California had said. He needed to make a decision on the job and quickly. If he decided to take it, he'd be on a plane within the week. Which meant a lot of things. Not the least of them being he'd have to put in his notice, cancel on the food critic, disappoint his friends, and leave Bria behind.

Bria.

He watched her closely as she slid the spoon into the chocolate mousse before she put it in her mouth. He felt a twinge low in his groin and was suddenly and totally irrationally jealous of the spoon. She winked at him when she noticed him watching and he had to look away, lest he do something completely inappropriate to her right in the middle of the restaurant with her grandmother sitting across from them. No. He'd get her alone later and do everything he'd been imagining all day, and he'd get some answers about what it was that was going on between them.

"Bria was telling me how busy you've been together."

Jax almost choked as he focused on Mona. "She told you what exactly?" He managed to force the question out and Mona only smiled sweetly in response.

"I was telling her all about the pictures I took and how I met some of your friends in the Grizzly Paw today and got to see the baby." Bria rolled her eyes, but there was laughter behind her action. "That's all I told her. She's being...troublesome."

"If you can't cause trouble at my age, when can you?" Mona winked and they all laughed. "Besides, I may be old, but as I told Bria earlier, I'm certainly not blind." Mona waved her spoon between the two of them. "And I know what I've been seeing here."

"Grandma, you know I love you more than anything, but you're not seeing anything."

Bria's words stung more than Jax cared to admit. He snuck a glance at her, and could see the hot blush that started at the back of her neck creep up.

"I don't think that's true at all," he said and Bria whipped her head up to stare at him. Her eyes were narrowed and shot warning signs at him. Warning signs he chose to ignore. "I think your grandmother is very clever and there's a whole lot going on here." Before she could protest, he took her head in his hands, and pulled her to his mouth to give her the most thorough kiss he could manage without ripping her clothes off and turning their PG-rated dinner into a very R-rated experience.

When he pulled back, her face was fully flushed, her chest heaved, and her eyes closed tightly. He was ready for her anger at exposing them so openly, but he was tired of hiding whatever it was they were doing and he was willing to deal with the backlash. But to his surprise, when Bria opened her eyes, they didn't flare with anger, but dark with barely restrained desire. Somewhere in the distance, he heard Mona's laugh and a clap of delight, but he was too focused on Bria and her reaction to focus on anything else.

She opened her mouth, but closed it again before she said anything. Finally, after what felt like a very long time in which Jax started to wonder whether he hadn't screwed everything up totally, Bria's lips twitched up in a smile that crept across her whole face and lit it up. "Okay, so there might be a little something going on." She gripped his hand under the table, and threaded her fingers through his.

Like a lovesick teenager, Jax's heart swelled. There was so much he didn't have answers for, including his completely unnatural reaction to this woman and his willingness to throw away everything he'd ever been or thought he was, after only a few weeks with her. He didn't know what the future for them looked like, or even how she really felt. But with her response, it had become a little bit clearer and at the moment, that was all he needed.

Mona laughed again. "Oh yes, there's definitely something going on, and I for one think it's fantastic. I also think it's long past time I turned in for the night."

"Grandma, you don't have to. It's only…oh, it's almost ten already."

Mona struggled to her feet and Jax couldn't help but notice the way she winced. Bria noticed it too and jumped to her feet, putting an arm around her grandma's shoulders. "I'll help you back to your room," she said. "And I'm going to make sure you take a pill. That's enough. You need some—"

"Nonsense." Mona shrugged her off. "You don't need to be looking after this old woman. You have a young man here who is patiently waiting to get you alone." Mona winked in Jax's direction and he made a mental note to have his pastry chef, Rose, bake her a special cake.

Bria looked torn, not sure what to do. Finally she looked at Mona. "You're sure?"

"Of course I'm sure. Go with Jax and have a nice evening." Bria pulled her into a hug and Jax could see Mona's mouth move as she whispered something to her granddaughter, but he couldn't be sure what she'd said. And when Bria pulled away, there was both a smile on her face and a tear in her eye.

BRIA STILL WASN'T sure she'd made the right decision sending Mona up to her room without accompanying her, but she had to trust that her grandmother would do the right thing. And besides that, she'd been so thrown for a loop when Jax had kissed her at the table, she wasn't sure she could trust any of her decisions anyway. She'd wanted to keep their relationship a secret for a bit longer, but not even she could explain why, so when Jax more or less outed them, her first response had been to get angry, but she wasn't.

She'd been relieved. It felt good to let others know what they were doing, even if she couldn't totally explain it herself. But more than that, if Jax was okay announcing they were together, then maybe he felt the same way she did. Maybe they did have a future or at least a chance together to have some sort of...well, something.

After Mona left, he hadn't wasted anytime getting her alone and up to his apartment, where they once again made love. Neither of them could get enough of the other, which made the sex between them almost unbearable in its intensity. She had no idea things could be that way with a man. Well, she had an idea of course, but she'd never really believed *she'd* experience it.

Afterwards, she curled up into the crook of his arm and let her eyes drift shut. It would be so easy to fall asleep with Jax next to her. And how would it be to wake up next to him, his arm holding her close? But she couldn't allow herself that luxury. Reluctantly, she slid down the bed and turned to roll out of the covers, but Jax's arm wrapped around her waist and pulled her back to him.

"Where are you going?"

She turned and kissed his shoulder. "I have to go. It's late."

"Stay."

One word, but said with so much intensity and longing that she closed her eyes and allowed herself to sink back against him.

"Please, Bria. I want you to stay."

He kissed her neck and she moaned.

"Jax, I can't. My grandma."

"Knows about us."

"But what is there to know?" The question popped out of her mouth before she even realized what she'd asked. "I mean, what is *us*? Is there something to know?"

She felt him tense behind her, and for a moment Bria was afraid she'd screwed everything up. But then his muscles relaxed again, and with the agility of a cat, he turned and flipped her so she was beneath him and his arms were braced on either side of her head. He stared down at her with so much intensity, her body vibrated. "I think there's a lot going on between us." He spoke slowly and so quietly she had to strain to hear him. "Don't you?"

She nodded because she didn't trust herself to speak.

"I think..." He dropped a kiss on her collarbone. "I don't want you to leave my bed." He kissed her again. "Ever."

It was one word, but it spoke volumes, especially because it was everything she'd been thinking and didn't dare say.

There was nothing she could say in return, so she answered him with a kiss of her own that ended the argument of anyone going anywhere.

. . .

MUCH LATER, Bria woke with a desperate thirst, so as carefully as she could, she slipped out from under his arm and pulled his t-shirt over her head. Before she left the room, she stopped to watch him sleep. He was even more amazing in the moonlight. The sheet had slipped and now his chest was exposed; the muscles looked even harder in slumber, but she knew from experience that as hard and chiseled as he looked, there was so much tenderness in the way he held her, touched her, spoke her name. Bria felt her chest tighten. It was an unfamiliar feeling, but she was certain she was falling for this man in a way that was going to leave one of them hurting. Hard.

But for the moment, it was all good. Better than good. She left him sleeping and padded out to the kitchen.

She flipped on the light over the stove so she could see what she was doing, and picked a cupboard at random in search of a water glass. As she reached for the glass, a letter caught her attention. It was addressed to Jax Carver.

She giggled at his last name the way she always did. It was more than a little ironic that a chef had the last name Carver. But she was being adolescent because whenever she brought it up to Jax, he looked at her as if she was crazy.

The return address caught her attention. Los Angeles, California. She knew she shouldn't and that it was none of her business, but Bria picked up the letter. It had been opened, so despite the voice in her head that screamed at her to mind her own business and not invade Jax's privacy, she slid the paper out and read the letter.

As she read, Bria felt all the blood drain from her face and hands until she thought she might drop the paper. She held the counter to support her shaking legs. Jax was moving to Los Angeles? In a few days?

She should have been excited for him. It was a great opportunity and anyone in his position would be crazy not to jump at it. But all Bria could think of was the words he'd said to her only a few hours ago. Had he been lying? Just saying things to get her to stay and sleep with him again? If he'd really meant any of the things he'd said, surely he couldn't be thinking of leaving without even telling her about it?

Not that he owed her anything, not really. But they were building something together. Weren't they? Wasn't that exactly what they'd been doing for the last few weeks? She felt a pain in her chest and it was hard to swallow. Or had she believed only what she wanted to?

Jax coughed in the other room and hurriedly she folded the paper and stuffed it back in the envelope. She found a glass, filled it from the sink and drank it down quickly before filling it again. Whatever it was that the letter meant, she couldn't say anything. She shouldn't have looked at it and she knew it. She had to wait for Jax to come to her.

With one last glance at the letter that was going to change everything, she flipped off the light and padded her way back to the bedroom. She slid back into the bed and curled up against Jax's warm body. In his slumber, Jax put his arm around her and pulled her even closer. "You're back," he mumbled into her hair. "Don't leave again."

She knew he was sleeping and he probably wouldn't even remember what he'd said come morning, but his choice of words caused a clench in her gut and she kissed the arm that held her close. "I won't," she said, knowing it was a promise she couldn't keep.

Chapter Thirteen

THERE WAS NO DOUBT, waking up with Bria in his arms felt right. Really right. It felt as though he wanted to do it every single day for the rest of his life. Which was a crazy thought, particularly because they'd only known each other a few short weeks and up until the moment she'd walked into his life, Jax was a sworn bachelor. But with Bria, it was different.

He couldn't explain it, but when she'd moved to leave the night before, he couldn't imagine spending the whole night without her warm body curled up against his and for the first time, he'd asked a woman to stay the night. It had been the best night, too. And he planned to repeat the situation as soon as possible.

He measured the grounds into the filter and filled the carafe as his eyes fell to the envelope on the counter. Damn.

He'd have to deal with that soon. It was a great opportunity, but now, more than ever, he couldn't imagine leaving the Springs. He pushed the letter away and finished preparing the rest of the breakfast tray. He was determined to give Bria a breakfast in bed that would encourage her to want a repeat in the very near future.

The problem with that plan was that for a chef, he had very little ingredients in his kitchen. He always prepared his meals in the restaurant or ate whatever was around, so he didn't really keep much stocked. He was able to dig up a bit of bread that he toasted and some apples he cut into slices and by the time the coffee was done brewing, he had a makeshift breakfast prepared.

With everything on a tray, he made his way down the hall, ready to wake Bria up with the aroma of fresh coffee but when he saw her with her silky black hair spread across the pillow, the smooth skin of her back exposed, and her chest rising and falling in slumber, he abandoned his plan in favor of a much better one.

Jax put the tray on his dresser and crawled across the mattress until he was on top of her. He dropped a kiss on her lips, moving slowly until her body started to stir beneath him and even in a half-asleep state, responded by answering his insistence.

"Mmm." Bria's arms came up around him to pull him down and he deepened the kiss. When he finally pulled back, she opened her eyes and smiled at him.

"Good morning, beautiful."

"With a wakeup call like that, it certainly is."

"I can't think of a better way to start the day." He picked up a strand of her hair and let it slide through his fingers.

"I can," she said with a mischievous grin. "But what is that amazing smell?"

He laughed, wishing he'd left the coffee in the kitchen so he could have her all to himself. Now that she knew there was caffeine to be had, he was pretty certain the raging hard-on in his shorts was going to have to wait. At least until she'd had some coffee.

But that was okay, because after the night they'd shared

and the things they'd said to each other, he was even more certain about the way things were headed and there would be plenty of time to show Bria exactly how he felt.

He put the tray on the bed and watched her eyes light up. "Breakfast?"

"Well, sort of. It'll have to do for now, until I can get you some proper food."

Bria broke off a piece of toast. "This is perfect, but do you know what I really want?"

Her mischievous smile told him everything he needed to know and Jax wasn't about to waste any more time pretending it was breakfast. He took the toast from her hand and slid over so he had her pinned underneath him. Exactly where he wanted her and would happily keep her all day.

IT WAS after noon by the time they managed to get put together enough to leave the apartment. After her breakfast that hadn't really happened, they'd moved to the shower, which turned into both of them back in bed, but finally when Bria's stomach rumbled so loud they could no longer ignore it, they agreed it was time to face real life and head down to the restaurant. Besides, she probably shouldn't neglect her grandmother completely. Something was a little bit off with Mona, and while Bria hoped it was as simple as her not taking her medicine regularly, Bria couldn't help but worry that there was more to it than that.

But she couldn't worry about that at the moment, not when she still needed to figure out what she was going to do about the letter she'd read and shouldn't have. She hadn't been able to sleep, and not just because Jax had done his best to fill her every moment with hot kisses on her skin that kept her body on high alert. Even when they'd finally taken a break from each other, and Jax had fallen into restful sleep, she hadn't been able to shut her mind off and stop thinking about what the letter meant.

Would he be leaving? If he took the job, he'd be leaving within the week, but how could he say the things he'd said to her and plan to leave, give up whatever it was they were creating together?

Bria didn't want to read too much into whatever was going on with Jax, but she was way past that point. There'd been a shift between them, and she was long past pretending that what they had wasn't special and at the very least, worthy of her asking him about the letter. He might be mad that she'd read it, but it was a risk she had to take. She was sick of playing games and being left in the dark. It was time for honesty.

And the sooner the better.

She pushed the button for the elevator, as Jax finished up locking the apartment and joined her. "What are you thinking about?" He ran his fingers down her cheek with a gentleness that caused a shiver to run through her. "You look a million miles away." He pulled her close, and kissed her, erasing all her worries away. At least for the moment.

When the elevator arrived, they shuffled onto it, not breaking their embrace.

"I assure you, I'm right here," she said. "And quite honestly, there's no place I'd rather be."

Bria couldn't believe the change within her in such a short time, and the power of one man to affect that change.

He pulled back, his face lit up with a grin that she knew she'd put there. They were so relaxed, she knew there was never a better time to bring up the letter. She opened her mouth to blurt it out but before she could say anything, her stomach let out a growl that damn near echoed in the space between them.

Jax laughed and gave her another squeeze before he released her. "I can think of one other place you might rather be," he said. "I better get you to the restaurant and get some food in you before you pass out from hunger."

She joined him in his laughter. "Okay. But, Jax?" Bria's laughter died and she turned serious. "After we eat, I have to talk to you about something, okay?"

"Of course." He raised an eyebrow and reached out to brush a strand of hair off her cheek and tuck it behind her ear. "Is everything okay? You look a little upset and after that night we just—"

"No," she said quickly. "I'm fine. Everything's fine. I just need to talk to you about something. Soon, okay?"

He smiled, and her stomach did a little flip. She wondered whether she'd ever get used to the way he looked at her. Hopefully not. And as she lost herself in another kiss, Bria tried to push out the worry that she'd finally let someone into her heart just to have him hurt her when he walked out.

"I'll tell you what," he said as they stepped off the elevator and walked down the hall. "After we eat and you check in with Mona, I'm all yours. Whatever you want to talk about, and then maybe a little less talking." His eyebrows wiggled in a way that was both totally ridiculous and completely sexy at the same time.

Despite the silliness of Jax's promise, Bria's insides burned with the expectation of later.

She looked up at him and bit her lip in the way she knew drove him crazy. "If you play your cards right, there will be—"

"Well, good morning." Bria froze at the sound of her grandma's voice and her instinct was to yank her hand away from Jax, who squeezed her tighter as if he read her mind. "Or should I say, good afternoon?"

They turned to see Mona giggle and blush like a schoolgirl as she approached. "Oh, don't bother pretending like it's not a very good afternoon for both of you. It's written all over your faces. You both have the look of someone who's had a very good—"

"Mona!" Jax held up his hands to ward off whatever it was she was going to say next, because whatever it was she was going to say, they were both equally sure they didn't want to hear it. "Please don't."

Mona momentarily looked taken aback, but she recovered quickly, the way she always did. "Well, I'm just saying. I'm not so old that I don't know that look well. Not that I—"

"Grandma. Please." Bria shook her head. "No more."

"Will you join us for lunch, Mona?"

She nodded and for a moment looked as though she was going to add in another comment. Wisely, she shut her mouth, linked arms with Bria and headed down the hall with them.

Bria tried to sneak a glance at her grandmother without drawing too much attention to it. She didn't seem to be in as much pain, and seemed to be much more like her old self. Maybe she'd finally broken down and taken her pills.

"Grandma, have you—"

"Jax!"

They all froze and then spun around in the direction of the voice that hollered from across the great hall. It started to look as if it might take a long time to get to the restaurant after all, and Bria's stomach got louder and louder all the time. But one look at Slade Black charging toward them was all it took for Bria's stomach to quiet down and a sick feeling took its place. She didn't know Slade very well, but she didn't need to be well acquainted with him to know that he was pissed about something.

"What's up?" Jax asked as he got closer. His voice didn't betray any concern, but Bria could see it in the way he tensed his shoulders that he was on guard, too. "You want to join us for—"

"No, I don't want to join you for anything," Slade snapped. "What I want is an explanation for this?" He slapped a newspaper in front of Jax and in the same motion, turned to glare at Bria. The sick feeling that had started moments before grew stronger.

She wanted to be wrong, but she was almost positive that when she looked at the paper that was now in Jax's hand that she wasn't going to like what she saw.

"What is this?"

"What the hell does it look like?"

What it looked like to Bria was a full color, front page photo of Slade proposing to Beth, with the headline: "Rock Star Ready To Say I Do." Even with the poor quality of the newsprint, it was easy for Bria to tell that it was her shot. The lighting was great, the romance of the mood captured perfectly. There was no doubt she'd taken the picture. The question was, how did it get in the newspaper?

Jax snapped the paper and took a closer look. "It looks like —what the hell?" He looked up at her, his face a question that quickly turned to anger when he saw the answer on her face. "Bria, how could you do this?"

"I knew it." Slade punched his fist into his open palm. "I don't know how I could have trusted you with—"

"Simon," Mona, who'd been silent until now, jumped in. She put her hand on Slade's arm in an effort to still him. "I'm sure that whatever you think Bria did—"

"I know she did it."

"Okay." Mona used her best grandmother voice and tried a different approach. "Why don't we ask Bria to explain before anyone jumps to conclusions."

All eyes turned to her. Mona's held the trust and assurance she expected from her grandma; Slade's were dark with anger, which was to be expected. But it was Jax's eyes she focused on. The same eyes that only moments before looked at her with promise and affection were now clouded with confusion and question. She knew she'd have to offer some sort of explanation, but how could she when she didn't even understand it herself?

"Well?" Slade grew impatient. "Did you take the picture or not?"

"I...well...yes." She finally spat the word out and followed it quickly with, "I took the picture but I didn't—"

"I knew it." Slade threw his hands in the air before he ran them through his hair. "Do you have any idea what you've done? We weren't going to announce the engagement until after I finished the album. This is my first solo effort and it's important for the media to be focused on the music, not on scrutinizing my new fiancée or the wedding, or any other detail from our private life. It's hard enough to always be in the public eye, but Beth didn't ask for this and neither did Jules. And now..." He spun and focused his gaze directly at Bria again. "Everyone knows. I don't suppose you have any idea what it's like to have the whole world know your news before you've had a chance to even tell your family."

She shook her head, completely unable to form any words that would make the situation better.

"No." Slade shook his head. "Of course you don't. Your type never does."

The word, and mostly the way he said it, stung. Bria looked to Jax but he only shook his head and looked away.

Mona came to her defense. "Type? Simon Black, you know I love you, and I know you're upset with Bria, but I hardly think being mean is going to fix anything."

"I'm sorry, Mona. I really am. But this..." He gestured to the paper Jax still held. "This is a betrayal that I can't even begin to explain. In my life, I've only been able to count good friends on one hand and Jax," he turned to focus on his friend,

"I trusted you. I came to you because I trusted you with this. And…" He shook his head.

If the whole situation hadn't been so crazy and out of control, Bria would have felt bad for Jax getting blamed for something he obviously had nothing to do with. And she did feel bad, but…it was all too much.

"Slade." Jax swallowed, his face hard and unreadable. "I had nothing to do with this. And I never would have brought her if I thought she would do something like this. I thought she was different."

Bria felt his words like a blow to the gut and if her grand-mother hadn't grabbed her hand and squeezed tight, she might have doubled over with the intensity of Jax's anger.

"That's not fair," she managed to say. "I didn't—"

"You took the pictures." Jax spun and waved the paper in the air. "You said you did it. And who else would have?" His eyes narrowed and she hardly recognized the man in front of her. "I know you were desperate to save your job, but this?" He shook his head and then in a much quieter voice, one laced with hurt, he asked, "How could you do it, Bria?"

There was no real answer to that question. Yes, she'd taken the picture but it was a reflex to her. Her camera was an extension of her body. She captured moments; it was what she did. She couldn't explain to them that it came as naturally as breathing. As for the photo in the newspaper, she had no idea how that happened. And there was no way she could reasonably explain something that she didn't have an explanation for. The only thing she could think of was that someone found the prints in her bag or…Cynthia.

"I…I…Jax." She reached out to Jax, needing to touch him and connect with him. He slipped away from her so quickly, she felt the loss keenly. "It wasn't me."

He looked at her with so much disappointment and hurt in his eyes that there was no way he could be the same man who only an hour ago had moved inside her, looked at her with what she obviously mistook for love, or at the very least, affection. She felt the beginning of a sob build in her, but she swallowed it back. She would not lose it. She could not lose control. Not yet.

"Bria, stop." He shook his head and looked away, which might have been worse than seeing the disappointment in his eyes. "Just stop. I can't do this right now."

"Jax. I took the pictures, yes. Of course. But I didn't give them to the newspaper." She looked to Slade, pleaded with his eyes for him to believe her. "I didn't. I swear."

There was a flicker of something in Slade's face, but before he could say anything, Jax tossed the newspaper to the ground. "I'm not listening to this anymore. Slade, I'm sorry, man. I really am."

He turned to leave. Without even listening to her explanation, he was just going to walk away. Bria stared at him in disbelief. The pain in her chest warred with anger toward Jax. He actually believed she could do something so distrustful as sell such intimate pictures to the newspaper. If he could believe that, he didn't know who she was and if he was willing to believe the worst about her, clearly everything she thought they had was nothing but a lie.

She wasn't going to stand there and let him walk away from her. Not without even hearing her out. She took her grandmother's hand in hers and gave it a gentle squeeze. "Come on, Grandma." Bria forced her voice to be strong. She would not let him know how he'd broken her. Never. "I don't need to stand here and listen to these accusations and neither do you."

She was beyond angry. She was hurt, and that was worse. But if Jax had turned around, reached out to her and tried to stop her from leaving, she would have stopped. She would have explained everything to him so he'd listen and they could clear up what was no more than a misunderstanding.

But he hadn't.

And it was more than a misunderstanding.

It was a betrayal.

To both of them.

Chapter Fourteen

IT'D BEEN ALMOST forty-eight hours since he'd been in bed with the woman he thought he might actually be falling for. And less than that since he'd learned she wasn't who he thought she was. How stupid could he have been? Jax turned around so quickly, he almost hit one of the prep cooks with the frying pan in his hand.

"Get out of my way," he growled, and the kid scurried away.

He knew he was being unreasonable but ever since Slade showed him that newspaper that showcased without a doubt what kind of woman Bria was, he'd felt as if his head might totally explode. How could he have been so wrong about her? He'd been willing to give up the chance of a lifetime for her. He'd been willing to actually try to make a relationship work. He'd never done that for anyone.

He laughed but there was nothing pleasant about the sound. It was a damn good thing he hadn't made that mistake. After he'd watched her walk away from him almost two days earlier, he'd gone straight back to his apartment, found the letter and he'd made the call. He left for California later that night. A fact he'd yet to share with anyone.

Part of him hoped if he waited, something would change. What that was, he wasn't sure.

But he'd waited and nothing had changed. And it looked more and more as though he'd be giving his notice on the way to the airport. Not that he'd given that a lot of thought. Hell, all he could think about was Bria. He hadn't seen her since everything imploded. At first, he'd assumed she'd left. Except she hadn't because he'd asked a few questions and figured out that she'd been seen at the pools. She was still there. His body reacted the way it always did when he let thoughts of her in. Only since their fight—or whatever it was—it wasn't just his body reacting, it was a damn annoying ache in his chest, too.

"Damn it." Jax stacked an empty saucepan with more force than he meant to, and the pile crashed to the counter. He needed to stop letting her affect him. It was over.

"Whoa. I don't know if that was necessary."

Jax spun around, ready to yell at whoever dared to interrupt him. He shut his mouth and swallowed his anger when he saw Carmen, a baby sling attached to her chest.

"Hey. Sorry, Carmen. I thought you were…" It didn't matter. If it had been anyone else, he would have yelled and they both knew it.

She smiled and rubbed her hand over the bulge that had to be the baby. "I didn't mean to interrupt whatever it was that you were doing. But I did want to talk to you. And Hunter here seems to like to walk, and you haven't really had a chance to meet him besides the other day in the Paw, but it was so busy and…anyway…here we are."

A flash of guilt hit him. Jax knew he was the only one of their friends who hadn't really made an effort to meet the baby. He'd planned to go over with Bria and take a gift, but…

He grabbed a towel and wiped his hands. "About that," he

said. "I'm sorry, Carmen. I meant to come by and meet him officially, but—"

"I know." He could see the concern in her eyes, which only made him feel worse about everything. "I heard about what happened. Or at least I heard Beth's side of the story."

Anger fueled up in him again at the idea that Beth had been hurt. She'd gone through enough; she didn't need the drama he'd helped bring to her. "I wish I could change it all," he said. "It's my fault and she's probably so upset. It's all—"

"She's not."

That stopped him. "What? How could she not be? Slade was furious." That was an understatement, but there was no point reliving the whole thing.

"He still is. Although I think Beth may have managed to calm him down a bit by now." Carmen laughed a little. "But Beth's not. Sure, she was a little upset, but mostly taken off guard, I think. But she understands that these things are going to happen. And besides, she really liked the picture. I think she was secretly happy to have a memory of it."

"But it shouldn't have ended up in the paper."

"No. But it did. And Beth knows it can't be undone. There's no point in being angry over it forever."

Her words hit him in the gut. Maybe she was right and he couldn't be angry forever, but it was easy for her to say. She wasn't the one who'd started to fall for someone who turned out to be a very different person than he thought she was. The Bria he'd come to know wouldn't betray trust like that, which just meant he hadn't come to know her at all and he'd been foolish to ever think he had. Worse, he'd almost gone against his entire philosophy and gotten attached. Almost. But there was a reason Jax kept moving on: people never failed to disappoint him.

"She's not a bad person, Jax."

He'd forgotten Carmen still stood there. He focused his

eyes on her, and she stared at him intensely, as if she could see exactly what he was thinking.

"Even if she did sell the photo, it doesn't mean she's a bad person."

"What do you mean, even if she *did* sell the photo? Of course she did."

Carmen shrugged and fussed with the baby briefly. "Did she say she did?"

"She said—" But she hadn't said she'd sold the picture. Only that she'd taken it. Jax shook his head. "She had to have done it. Who else would have?"

"Like I said, even if she did it, which I have trouble believing, it doesn't have to be a deal breaker."

He let her words sink in, but he didn't want to think about what Carmen'd said. He didn't want to think anymore at all. He just wanted to get away and forget about everything. And the only way he was going to be able to do that was to appease Carmen. He wiped his hands again and walked around the counter to meet the baby properly.

"THAT'S ENOUGH."

Mona's sharp voice cut through the air and permeated the blanket Bria had tugged over her head. Maybe if she ignored her, she'd go away.

"Get up." The blanket was yanked off her head, letting in the harsh light and her grandmother's pointed words. "Enough is enough and I will not have you lying around here sulking forever."

Bria reached out for the blanket, but Mona held it just out of reach. "I want to sleep."

"No." Mona ripped the covers off completely and Bria had no choice but to sit up.

She crossed her arms like a pouty child. "Grandma, leave me alone."

"I will not. This has gone on long enough. It's time you get up and figure out what you're going to do."

Bria flopped back on the bed. "I don't want to."

She was aware she was being ridiculous, but she didn't care. She didn't care about anything except sleeping. And even that wasn't entirely true. She hadn't properly slept for the last few days. She hadn't done anything and it made her crazy. This was exactly why she'd never bothered with a man before, not really. What was the point of finally opening your heart when it was only going to be trampled on?

He didn't believe her. Not only that, he didn't even care enough to listen to her.

It was that realization that kept her up. She couldn't turn off her brain long enough to forget the way Jax had looked at her when he thought she'd betrayed their trust. But he hadn't even tried to understand. And that was what broke her heart.

"Bria." Mona's tone shifted and softened, and she eased herself down to the bed. When she reached out and stroked her hair, Bria almost cried. She'd been able to hold herself together, but the pain was real and it hurt more than she ever could have thought. She swallowed hard and tried to stuff her feelings down. She knew she couldn't stay in the hotel room forever and avoid life. But it seemed like the easiest course of action. At least for the moment. "Look at me, sweetheart," Mona persisted.

After a moment, she opened her eyes and looked at her grandmother. "I'm sorry, Grandma. I am. I just…"

"It's okay. But I do need you to get out of bed."

"Why?" She shook her head like a child. "Why can't I just stay here forever?"

"I'm not even going to answer that." Mona rolled her eyes and her voice hardened. "But I am going to tell you that it's time you stopped acting like a victim. Never in your life have you ever been a victim, and I'm not about to let you start now."

"Grandma, I—"

"I mean it. My Bria would not be sulking around like her world had come to an end."

"Well, it—"

Bria was silenced by Mona's harsh look. "Your world has not come to an end."

It was Bria's turn to roll her eyes, even though she knew her grandmother was right. But wasn't she allowed to feel sorry for herself, even a little bit? "What would you prefer I do, Grandma? Jax was different. I really like...I liked him. A lot."

"You don't still like him?"

Bria pulled her knees into her chest. "It doesn't matter."

"To hell it doesn't. You are a Sheridan. And Sheridan women do not sit back and let their life happen to them. A strong woman knows what she wants and goes after it. If you like, or dare I say, love Jax Carver, you need to get up out of this bed and go fight for what you want. Make him listen to your side of things. Make him understand, Bria. And if he still can't see what's right in front of him, then he wasn't worth all this hardship in the first place. But at least you'll know you tried."

While her grandmother ranted the way only Mona could, Bria listened. She absorbed every word and for a moment even felt as if Mona had a point. She'd never been the type of person to sit back and accept situations. She'd always fought for what she believed in and what was important. Always. Why should this situation be any different? Bria bit her bottom lip and nodded slightly before she got to her feet.

"You're right, Grandma," she said. "Everything you said is right on."

"That's my girl." Mona stood next to her and tugged her sweater down into place with a self-satisfied grin.

Bria swallowed hard. She knew what she should do. "But I can't do it." She shook her head sadly, crossed the room and pulled her suitcase from the closet. Sometimes knowing what you *should* do was too different from what you *could* do.

HE WAS ALMOST down the mountain when Jax passed the gravel side road that brought back so many memories of Bria. Only a few days ago, he'd considered it *their spot*. He paused and lifted his foot from the gas pedal. He could turn around and find her, see whether she was still a guest, and if not, find out where she went, hunt her down, pull her into his arms and kiss those sweet lips until everything between them was okay again.

But he couldn't.

Everything was different now and it was long past time for him to move on. He knew it'd been a mistake to stay in Cedar Springs as long as he had, and the whole catastrophe with the photos only proved it. No. It was too late to go back.

He kept driving, right down the main street of town. He focused on the road in front of him, not allowing himself to look at any of the familiar places—or the people who went with them —that had somehow over the months come to feel like home. He swallowed hard against the lump in his throat that protested his leaving. He'd never been nostalgic when he'd moved before. He'd never once felt as though maybe he was making a mistake.

But he'd never had a Bria before.

The thought was ridiculous in itself, considering Bria belonged there just about as much as he did.

But if he really believed that, then why did he feel so terrible? It was all wrong. Everything about what he was doing was wrong and he knew it.

Jax ignored the growing feeling of unease as he guided his truck out of town and down the highway. He'd made arrangements to have his truck picked up after his flight left and delivered to Archer at the Grizzly Paw. He'd put it to good use hunting or gathering wood or some such thing. It wouldn't matter.

He passed a sign for the airport. In less than thirty minutes, he'd be at the gate, ready to get on a plane and start a new life. Again. In the past, it had always been exciting. This was different.

His cell phone rang and pulled him out of what was quickly becoming a full-fledged funk. He answered it on reflex and instantly wished he hadn't.

"What the hell is this?" Dylan's voice rang out over the speakerphone in the truck. Jax didn't even try to pretend that he didn't know what his friend was talking about. He would have seen his resignation letter by now. "You can't do this, Jax. We have Augustus coming tonight. Tonight! What the hell am I going to do? I can't serve him take-out, Jax."

"Let Brent cook. He's good and—"

"Are you kidding? Please tell me you're kidding. Maybe you're drunk. Don't drink and drive, Jax. Get the hell back here right now."

If the whole situation hadn't been so screwed up, Jax would have laughed at his friend's ranting. As it was, it wasn't funny because Jax knew he'd done it to Dylan. And he felt like shit about it.

"I'm sorry," he said again. "I really am."

There was a silence on the other end, with only the hum of the truck filling the air and for a moment, Jax thought he'd been disconnected. When Dylan finally spoke again, his voice was different. Resigned. "Don't do this, man. You don't really want to leave. I can't believe that."

Jax was going to spout off the list of reasons he'd created in an effort to explain his decision, but when he opened his mouth, nothing came out. He shook his head even though Dylan couldn't see him. The truth was, Dylan was right. He didn't want to leave. But even more, he didn't want to face what was left for him in Cedar Springs. Or more accurately, not left for him.

"Jax?"

"I'm sorry, man. I just can't stay."

"Because of Bria." It wasn't a question, but it didn't have to be. "Carmen told me she saw you earlier today."

"Did she?" Jax navigated the truck to the shoulder on the highway. It was getting harder to concentrate on the road while he had this conversation.

"She did. And she told me you were upset. Heartbroken, even."

"I don't know about—"

"Whatever. You like her."

Jax couldn't argue with that. He did. Despite everything in him telling him to keep his distance from Bria, he couldn't. She compelled him in a way no other woman ever had. He liked her. A lot. Maybe he was even starting to love her. And wasn't that the real problem? He slammed his fist against the steering wheel. "So what if I do?"

"Then do something about it."

Jax sighed and closed his eyes before he leaned his head back on the seat. There was nothing to be done. Whatever had happened or not happened with the photos, he'd been a jerk about it all. He'd walked away from her without a second glance. The look in her eyes haunted him. Bria wouldn't forgive him. He'd screwed it up. Bad.

"I gotta go, Dylan. I'm sorry about the critic."

"Jax. Don't—"

He dropped the cell on the seat next to him, feeling like a class-A jackass. Dylan didn't deserve his attitude, and he certainly didn't deserve to lose out on the opportunity of the critic just because his head chef had messed up his personal life beyond belief. He shook his head and put the truck back into gear before he eased his way back on the highway. It was too late now, anyway, he told himself.

Besides, even if he could put the whole Bria thing behind him, and was going to cook for the critic, he didn't have anything planned. He'd done a great job of totally ignoring his career and his responsibilities at the Springs, and had barely given the menu a second thought. And once Archer told him there was no venison, the only plan he sort of had went out the window. So really, it wasn't his fault.

But even with that circular logic, Jax still couldn't shake the guilt, and the overwhelming sense that he was not only letting everyone down, he was making a really big mistake while he was doing it.

JAX PULLED into the parking lot and looked at his watch again: 4:00 p.m. He had thirty minutes to meet his flight. Plenty of time. He also had two hours to cook the meal of his life for the food critic who could potentially make his career. He stared at the steering wheel. It was a big choice. One he'd thought he'd made.

But he couldn't get the conversation with Dylan out of his head. Let alone the memory of Bria's smile, the way her eyes shone when she spoke about photography, her soft lips on his, her body under his as he—no. He had to stop. He'd never made a decision for a woman before, and he wasn't about to start now. But he did have a decision to make and the more he let himself think about the choice, the harder it was to make.

It had seemed so cut-and-dry earlier. He had to leave. Start over somewhere where nobody knew him and he wouldn't have the constant reminder of what he almost had with Bria, and then lost. Never mind the chance-of-a-lifetime job opportunity. He'd be a fool to turn it down. His own kitchen, full creative control, and executive chef at one of the hottest restaurants today.

It sounded awfully familiar. It sounded like what he already had.

Except California didn't have Bria.

Hell, the Springs probably didn't have Bria anymore because of the way he handled things. For all he knew, she was gone on to the next assignment. Damn, he didn't even know where she called home. Or if she called anywhere home. They'd talked about a lot of things, but a home wasn't one of them. For either of them. Why was that?

Jax scrubbed a hand over his face. He knew what that was. At least for him, he didn't talk about where his home was because for him, he'd already been home. The Springs resort, the whole town of Cedar Springs, and everyone in it had been the closest thing he'd ever had to a home. No, it really was home. Why hadn't he seen that before?

He glanced at the airport terminal again. He could be on the plane in a little under an hour.

Or.

He swiveled around to look at the exit for the highway. He could be back at the Springs, fighting for the life he wanted and could still have.

Before he could make the decision either way, his phone rang and he grabbed it.

"I got it." Archer's voice sounded far away, the line full of static.

"Got what?" Jax glanced between his two choices again.

"It's not venison. I know that's what you wanted, but I get the next best thing. A perfect, beautiful rainbow trout. I actually got a few, because I'm that good." Jax could hear the laughter in his friend's voice. "I know I said I couldn't find a minute to get out, but I needed to get away, so I made a fishing trip happen and…anyway, it doesn't matter. What matters is that there's a fresh and absolutely amazing prime fish headed your way and that critic is going to be totally blown away."

A trout? Bria said her favorite meal would be fish. Jax's mind spun and he focused on what Archer was saying.

"I've tasted your trout before, man. And it doesn't get any more Rocky Mountain. My mouth is watering just thinking about the magic you can work with this, man. It's going to be—"

"Archer. Whoa. I wasn't…" He let his protests die on his tongue. He wasn't going to what? Was he really about to tell this guy who'd been his best friend for the last few months, and possibly the best friend he'd ever had, that his efforts had been wasted? He could. Nothing stopped him from telling Archer the truth: that he was leaving and his friendship and the fact that he'd gone out of his way to secure the freshest ingredients for him because it was good for Jax's career meant nothing. But Jax would be lying. Because it did mean something. It meant a lot.

"You weren't going to what?" Still, Jax couldn't bring himself to tell Archer the truth. "Jax? Do not tell me that you don't need this fish because so help me, I'm still at the river, about to gut and—"

"No." Suddenly Jax knew exactly what he needed to say. "I don't need *a* fish." He smiled as he imagined the way Archer would be flipping out on the other end of the line. "I need two." He fired up the engine, slammed the gearshift into reverse, backed out of the parking lot and headed back to the highway. "How fast can you get them to the restaurant for me?" Jax glanced at the dashboard clock. He had time. He had enough time to get back into the kitchen and save his career, even if there was no hope left for his relationship.

He felt a pang in his chest at the idea that Bria wouldn't be there when he got back. But he didn't have time to dwell on it. "I have to call Dylan," he told his buddy. "You just focus on getting out of the woods and back to the hotel for me."

They signed off and with a fresh resolve, a little bit of hope deep down, and a grin from ear to ear, Jax dialed Dylan's number and pressed his foot to the gas.

Chapter Fifteen

BRIA TOOK A DEEP BREATH, pulled her hair back off her shoulders and braced herself for what she was about to do. Slade and Beth sat with their backs to her, tucked into a corner by a fountain in the main hall. Exactly where she'd told Beth she'd like to meet with them. It was private enough for what Bria wanted to do and public enough that Slade would probably behave himself and not yell at her. Not that a semi-public place would prevent all yelling, but she had to hope it would help.

She rolled her suitcase behind her, left it next to a pillar, clutched her camera bag to her chest and with one final breath, stepped in front of the couple.

"Bria." There was warmth in Beth's eyes and her smile when she greeted her. For a moment, Bria felt the tension leave her shoulders, but as soon as she looked over at Slade, it returned. His mouth was set in a firm line; his jaw clenched as he swallowed hard, obviously working to control his temper.

"Thank you for meeting with me," Bria said quickly, avoiding Slade's eyes. She sat across from them and pulled her camera bag to her lap. "I know you didn't have to, what with everything that...well, I appreciate it."

"Of course." Beth smiled again and gave Slade a nudge with her elbow. "Don't mind him. He's just grouchy."

Slade opened his mouth to protest, but closed it again and sat back in his seat.

There was no point wasting any more time, and as far as Bria was concerned, the faster she got this little meeting over with and got out of there, the better. She'd packed her bags, said her goodbye's to her grandma, who assured her she'd be heading home soon, too. And now that the decision had been made to leave, she wanted to do it as soon as she could. But she couldn't leave without taking care of one more thing.

"I know I can't change your mind about what happened," Bria started.

"No," Slade said. "You can't."

"Slade." Beth gave her fiancé a dirty look before she returned her kind gaze to Bria.

"Don't worry, I'm not going to try to convince you that I had nothing to do with what happened." She unzipped her camera bag and pulled out the packet. "Because the fact is, I did take the picture. In fact, I took a whole bunch of pictures." Slade opened his mouth again, and Bria continued quickly. "And I probably shouldn't have. But you have to understand that it's what I do. I take pictures of beautiful things...and beautiful people," she added. "I was honored to be able to help in even a small way with what was a very special night for you both, and I hope you understand that I would never purposely try to hurt either of you. But I saw an amazing moment, and I picked up my camera. I never intended for those pictures to be sold or given to the press in any way."

"Then what did you expect to happen?"

Bria swallowed hard and looked Slade straight in the eyes. "I expected that I'd capture a once-in-a-lifetime moment. One that you might want to remember forever." She handed the packet to Slade.

He stared at the envelope in his hands for a moment before he looked up at Bria. "What's this?"

"That's your moment." She smiled, and it was genuine because she knew what was inside. The pictures were beautiful. More than beautiful, they were the best photos she'd ever taken and it had nothing to do with her but everything to do with the couple she'd photographed.

Slade glanced down with a wary eye before he looked at her again.

"Open them." Beth almost jumped out of her seat and reached for the envelope before Slade had a chance to open it himself. "I can't believe..." Beth's words trailed away as she stared at the picture in her hand. "This is..." She looked up at Bria and back to the pictures. "Oh my goodness." Beth's hand flew to her mouth, and Bria saw the tears form in the other woman's eyes. She didn't blame her for getting emotional. When Bria looked at the pictures, she'd felt the same way and she wasn't the subject of them. She'd probably never be the subject of something so special and romantic, she thought with a bitter edge. She squeezed her eyes shut for a second, not allowing the thoughts of Jax to take purchase in her head. Not again.

"That's all of them," she said. "Including the one that made it into the paper. And for the record," she added quickly when Slade's head jerked up again. "I didn't do it. In fact, I never meant to even have the pictures printed when I developed all the shots of the Springs. The only thing I can think of was that they were all on the stick that I took to the shop to have processed. I was a bit distracted and..." That was an understatement. It was a miracle Bria had been able to function with all the time she'd spent with Jax, in his bed and in her heart. She shook her head and forced a smile she didn't feel

"Anyway, it was an accident. I was going to put them all on a USB stick and give them to you. They're yours—they always were."

Beth continued to flip through the stack. The tears fell freely down her cheeks now. "I can't believe you did this."

"I know, I know." Bria held up her hands in defense. "I shouldn't have done it, but it's like a reflex with me. I can't help it."

"No." Beth shook her head. "That's not what I meant. They're absolutely amazing. Thank you."

"What?" She'd expected a lot of things from the couple, but gratitude was not one of them. A quick glance at Slade told her the gratitude was definitely one-sided. She'd never be able to explain her side of the story to him.

Or Jax.

Again, she pushed the thought of Jax out of her head. It was too late for all that.

"Anyway, I should get going." Now that she'd taken care of this one last detail, she was done. Nothing kept her at the Springs, or more to the point—no one.

She stood to go, but Slade's hand shot out and grabbed her arm to still her. "Wait."

Bria froze and locked eyes with the rocker. She waited for him to continue.

"Did you say you had the pictures printed at the shop? What shop?"

It took Bria a few moments to process the question. "The general store down in town. As far as I know, it's the only place in Cedar Springs that will still print pictures. At least, that's what Jax said." Just saying his name was like a knife to her heart. She blinked back the pain and continued. "I know it's kind of old-fashioned, but that's how I like to work. I always go through physical prints of my shots before I submit anything.

I'm probably the most photo printing business Cynthia's had in—"

She froze. She hadn't meant to say anything.

"Did you say Cynthia?" Beth asked.

Bria nodded. She'd always known it had to have been the redhead who'd sold the photo. She would've been the only other person who'd see them. It wouldn't have been very difficult to run another set of pictures, or even just take one. It had always been the only explanation and Bria knew it. She also didn't feel like causing trouble for someone else. Especially someone who lived in town.

"That makes sense, Slade." Beth turned to her man and grabbed his hand. "I knew Bria didn't do it."

Wait. How would she have known that?

"You just don't look like the type," she said as way of explanation, as if she'd read Bria's mind. "And I'm a pretty good judge of character. And now that you mentioned Cynthia, that all makes perfect sense. She probably couldn't have helped herself."

"She probably did it to get back at me," Bria said wryly. "She didn't seem very happy that I was spending time with Jax." A lot of time. But she didn't bother adding that. "I don't think she liked me much."

Beth laughed. "Maybe not. Cynthia can be pretty territorial with her men, but she's not the type to do something like this for revenge. She needs money. Things have been hard lately with her mom being sick. I bet she saw an opportunity to pay a few bills, and took it."

Bria tilted her head and assessed the other woman. "And you're not mad?"

"Like hell we're—"

Beth put a hand on Slade's arm to still him. "No. We're not." She emphasized the words. "This is par for the course when it comes to living in the public eye. I should probably get used to it, right?"

"But not our—"

"It doesn't matter, Slade. It happened. Besides, they're beautiful pictures. It's not like we were caught with our pants down or anything." They both shut their mouths and looked quickly at Bria.

Stunned, she laughed. "Hey, I don't know what you did after we left, but I assure you those are the only pictures I got."

With the tense moment diffused, Bria slumped back in her seat and relaxed a bit. She could never have imagined how well the couple would react. Even with Slade's defensiveness, it was easy to see he was just trying to protect Beth, and Bria could appreciate that. Even if it made her green with envy.

"I should get going." Bria pushed herself out of the chair. "I hope you enjoy the pictures. It truly was the most beautiful thing I've ever seen. I hope you two are very happy together." Bria felt a tear of her own build in her eyes, and she blinked hard to keep it at bay.

Beth jumped to her feet and pulled her into a hug. "Thank you so much. Can we reach you through Jax? In case we need more pictures? Like maybe engagement pictures." She let go of Bria and wiggled her eyebrows at Slade, who just shook his head with a laugh.

"Whatever."

Bria was glad she wasn't looking at her anymore because she didn't want Beth to see the pain in her eyes that she no longer could try to hide. "Jax won't have my number," she said quietly. "Here." She dropped a business card on the table in front of her even though she had no intention to photograph them again. "I have to go."

She grabbed her camera bag and hustled out of there before she could say another word or make a fool of herself even further. They didn't need to know the details of what had happened between her and Jax. Especially when she couldn't explain it herself. She thought they'd had something they hadn't. Period.

IT HAD BEEN A WHIRLWIND EVENING. Jax had arrived in the kitchen only moments before Archer had with his perfect and extraordinarily fresh trout. With fish this fresh, it really wouldn't need much to make it food-critic worthy. But Jax was fully prepared to do everything he could to make sure that Augustus loved his meal and had nothing but positive things to say about it and the Springs.

There was no time to talk to Archer, but he promised to come down to the Grizzly Paw for what would definitely be a celebratory drink. He didn't bother mentioning that he'd also be drowning his sorrows and his stupidity for screwing things up with Bria, too. It didn't matter; there'd be time to rehash his screwed-up life later.

After Archer left, everyone left Jax alone to create. His sous chef was on hand and Brent was amazing at reading his mind, getting him the ingredients he needed, before he even asked. With Brent at his side, Jax was pretty sure the two of them could be a formidable force in the culinary world. Something else to think about later, and he'd have plenty of time to think about the future of his career at the Stillwater, right there at the Springs, since the one thing Jax could be sure of in that moment was that he wasn't going anywhere. He felt at home in that kitchen. Hell, he was home. Everything else would figure itself out. And by everything else, he meant Bria.

Damn. Thoughts of her kept pushing their way into his consciousness. Instead of trying to force him to forget her, Jax used the thoughts to fuel him. He channeled her smile, her sweet smell, and the way she licked her lips when she got excited, and he focused all of that energy into his cooking the trout as if he cooked it for her. Her favorite meal.

By the time Dylan and Trent came in to inform him that Augustus had arrived and was ready for his meal whenever Jax was, he was more than ready. Everything had come together perfectly. He placed the whole grilled trout on top of a bed of lemon-pepper mixed greens, and topped it with a freshly prepared lemon butter that instantly melted along the crisp skin of the fish. He garnished with a spring pea puree and a slice of lemon twisted elegantly. It was perfectly put together, artfully presented, and the aroma made everyone's mouth water.

"I'm as ready as I'm going to get, man." Jax set the plate in the window. "Take it."

"It looks amazing," Trent said. "If he doesn't love it, he's—"

"He'll like it." Jax nodded, unwilling to let any negative thoughts in.

"Yes, he will," Trent agreed. "Here we go."

As soon as Trent took the plate out to the dining room, Jax leaned back against the counter, closed his eyes and let out a long breath he didn't realize he'd been holding.

"I'm glad you came back, man. Really." Jax opened his eyes and looked at Dylan. "I don't know what changed your mind, but I'm sure glad you did."

"I know you needed this. A positive critical review will really help the Springs." Jax wiped down his prep area. He didn't usually make too much of a mess when he cooked, but he liked an immaculate kitchen.

"Yes, it will. But that's not what I'm talking about."

Jax stopped cleaning and looked at his friend.

"I would've missed you, man. And that's all I'm saying about that."

They laughed and shared a quick man-hug, back slap

before they retreated to opposite ends of the counter again. Jax continued to clean and waited for Dylan to say more, because he knew he would. After a moment, Dylan spoke again. "Are you going to tell me who that one's for?" Jax looked up; Dylan pointed to the second perfectly prepared and presented rainbow trout dish. An exact duplicate of the one he'd sent out to Augustus. The one he'd prepared for Bria, even if she'd never taste it.

Jax shrugged, unwilling to answer the question. They fell into silence again, before Dylan finally asked the question Jax had been waiting for.

"The reason you came back, was it really for the critic or for her?" There was no judgment in his voice and Jax knew either way, Dylan wouldn't care why he'd chosen to stay, but it was important to Jax that he knew the truth.

"Neither," he said after a moment.

Dylan crossed his arms over his chest. "Neither?"

It had taken Jax longer to come to such a simple reasoning and he was almost embarrassed to tell Dylan the truth, only because he should have figured it out long before now. "No. I came back for me. I'm sick of moving on and there'll never be a better opportunity than the one that's right here. Besides, this is my home and I can't say I've felt like I've ever really had a home."

Across the counter, Dylan listened and nodded.

"Does that sound stupid?" Jax asked the question, but he really didn't care about the answer either way.

"No. It doesn't because you are home, buddy. And we've got something here that Los Angeles can't even come close to."

Jax laughed. It felt good after too many days of hurting. He still had a long way to go, but he was on the mend, and he knew that now. "Oh yeah? What's that?"

"Snow, of course. You know there's nothing like a good old winter in the mountains."

"Ha. Isn't that the truth? Thank God it's spring and I don't have to deal with that for a few months. Maybe I'll reevaluate by then."

"No deal. You're here for good now. I'm going to put that in your contract. And hasn't anyone told you? It can snow at any time up here. It doesn't have to be winter."

Jax groaned, but he didn't care. Not really. Just knowing he'd be calling the resort and the town of Cedar Springs home made him feel lighter than he had in ages. The only other time he'd been so comfortable was with Bria. And the thought of her, likely in a car hurtling down the highway or on a plane flying God knew where away from him, caused a physical ache in his chest that not only dampened the good feelings he had about staying, but pretty much doused them completely.

Without realizing it, he let his gaze drift to the untouched meal on the counter.

"So what are you going to do about Bria?"

The question took him off guard. Dylan stared at him as he waited for an answer.

"It's written all over your face, Jax. And you can ask Carmen, I'm not the most sensitive guy around, but I'm not completely bereft of emotions, and I can see it on you. You love her."

Love? It was a strong word and a strong feeling for someone he hadn't known very long, or even spent that much time with. "I don't know about—"

"Say what you want, but I know a heartsick fool when I see one, and that's exactly what you are. Hell, you almost threw it all away because of a little argument. If that's not a sign of heartsick, I don't know what is."

"I didn't…" There was no point finishing the sentence. Jax didn't even believe his own argument. "Okay, even if I did. Does it even matter?"

Dylan didn't answer but instead gave him a look as if he was totally crazy.

"What?"

"It matters," he said simply.

"She's gone."

"Is she?"

Chapter Sixteen

SHE'D ALMOST MADE it out the front door to the taxi she'd had the woman at the front desk call for her. Almost.

"Bria?" She froze and considered not turning around. She could ignore Carmen and just keep walking. It would be so easy. Bria looked to the large oversized glass doors that led to her freedom from the place she'd come to love and hate in almost equal measure. She turned.

"I'm glad I caught you." Carmen walked quickly toward her, a sling strapped to her chest that held a bundle that could only be little Hunter. She'd seen the baby the other day, but the scene in the Grizzly Paw had been a chaotic meeting of what seemed like everybody in town, all celebrating and jostling to see the new mom and her son. It definitely wasn't Bria's scene, particularly when she didn't really know any of them. They were Jax's friends. Or were, or…it didn't matter. She had no need to get to know them now. Even though they'd all seemed like really nice, genuine people. The type of people she'd love to have been friends with. "I heard you were leaving and I can't let you leave without letting me thank you properly."

"You don't need to do that." And she meant it, because if

Carmen planned to thank her properly, no doubt that meant it was going to take some time and Bria would not be leaving as soon as she'd like. Which would be at that exact moment if she could help it.

"I do," Carmen insisted. "Besides, you haven't really had a chance to get to know Hunter and after everything you did for me, and him, I need a picture of the two of you together."

Instinctively, Bria backed up half a step and held her hands up in front of her. She didn't do babies. That kind of went with not having any friends who'd ever been pregnant; she'd never had any friends who had babies. She'd never even babysat as a teenager because her mother thought it was beneath her to have a daughter who cared for other people's children. And she didn't need anything else making it more difficult to leave. She just needed to get out. "No, really, Carmen. It's fine and I should probably get going. I have a cab waiting and I don't want to make them wait too long."

"Nonsense." Carmen waved away her concerns. "That's just Bernie. He's the only cabbie in town and he's just as happy to sit and snooze than to drive you somewhere. Where are you going anyway?" She grabbed Bria's arm and led her toward a low leather bench next to one of the water feature pools in the lobby. "It doesn't matter. It can wait, right?" Bria almost protested, but from her last experience with the woman, it was clear that Carmen was a force and it was just easier to go along with it than try to fix it. "Kari," Carmen called over her shoulder to the woman at the front desk, who looked vaguely familiar. "Could you tell Bernie he can go?"

"What?" Bria spun around as best she could with Carmen's surprisingly strong grip on her arm. "No. I'm going to be going right away. Kari?" The pretty little brunette at the desk pretended as if she hadn't heard her, but there was no way she hadn't. And then she remembered where she'd seen her before. At the Grizzly Paw, as one of the "gang." She'd been with the cop, Rhys, if she remembered correctly. It didn't matter, because she was more or less being abducted and that cop was nowhere to be seen and even if he was, Bria had the strange suspicion it wouldn't matter.

"Sit down," Carmen commanded with a sweet smile. Before Bria could protest again, she was sitting on the leather bench, and the baby was being pressed into her arms.

Her instinct was to pull away, but fortunately she stopped herself. "Wait." Her eyes flew up to meet Carmen's. "Shouldn't I wash my hands or something first? I mean, they—"

"Are just fine," Carmen finished for her. "He's a baby—he's not going to break. Just hold him."

Bria looked down into a pair of the bluest eyes she'd ever seen. Hunter was awake and stared straight up at her. He pressed his tiny little bow lips together before they opened into a perfect *O* as he yawned. Something in her chest released, and a feeling Bria had never had washed through her entire body, starting at her head and went all the way down to her toes. She adjusted him so he was settled more firmly in the crook of her left arm and she adjusted his blanket, pulling it back so she could see his unbelievably small hand. Hunter's fingers reflexively flexed and stretched in the cooler air and Bria slipped her index finger in his palm so he could wrap his hand around it.

"Oh my," she cooed. "You have a grip just like your mother's." Somewhere in the background, Bria heard Carmen laugh, but it sounded very far away, because she was so taken by the perfect little creature in her arms. He yawned again and closed his eyes. As if she'd done it forever, she gently swayed from side to side to rock him to sleep. "You are just the sweetest thing I've ever seen," she told him quietly and surprising even herself, she bent down and put a kiss on his forehead and the dusting of hair there.

"You're a natural."

Still in a baby trance, it took a second for the voice to

register with Bria. It wasn't Carmen who'd spoken. Slowly, not trusting herself, she looked up.

"Hi," Jax said softly.

Bria glanced around to search for Carmen.

"Don't worry, she's right there. I thought it might be safer to talk to you like this."

She looked down at the baby and then back to Jax, who watched her with a wary expression. "Safer?"

"I figured if you were holding a baby you couldn't yell at me or hit me." His lips twitched up in a sort of smile and Bria was even more confused.

"I don't understand. You…we…what is going on?"

With her hands occupied, Jax tentatively slid his hand on her knee. A spark shot through her traitorous body. "I'm trying to apologize."

"For what?" Bria's mind couldn't keep up with what was happening and she didn't dare hope that he was going to say what she'd hoped he would. She couldn't look at Jax. Her stomach flipped and her chest squeezed too tightly for her to get a breath in when she looked at him. It was safer to stare at the baby. The peaceful, sleeping, innocent baby who she suddenly hoped with a passion that startled her would never have to experience any type of heartache in his life.

"I'm not doing this right," Jax said. "I'm sorry for that too. Hell, I'm sorry for a lot of things. Bria, can you look at me?"

She shook her head. She couldn't. Not yet. She didn't even know what to say to him. Never in her entire life had a man turned her so inside out before. She was a strong woman. She didn't compromise for anyone. Ever. So why was she feeling as though if she looked at him, she would burst into tears? Why did her heart feel as if it would absolutely shatter if she let it?

"Okay." Jax squeezed her knee. "I don't blame you. I really don't. I was a total jerk and I screwed up and…dammit, Bria, you have to look at me." There was something in his voice. It was so…broken, as if just maybe he hurt the same way she did. But that was ridiculous. He'd chosen this. Bria squeezed her eyes shut. No. She refused to believe that he was hurting, too. He did this. He left her there, abandoned her and whatever it was they were building. A relationship.

It was a relationship that they were building and as much as it hurt to admit that, even to herself while he sat in front of her, his hand on her knee, trying to make her look at him, that's what it was. *Was.* Something real. Or at least the beginning of something real. Of something that could be something. That's why it all hurt so goddamn much. She opened her eyes, took one more look at the sleeping infant in her arms and looked up, searching for Carmen's watchful gaze. She nodded at the woman and Carmen rushed over to take Hunter. As the baby was lifted from her arms, she felt a pinch of loss and an emptiness she never would have expected.

Carmen popped him back into the snuggly on her chest and with a quick glance at both of them, she beat a hasty retreat. It was only after she was gone that Bria dared to look at the man in front of her.

The moment their eyes connected, she was instantly taken aback. It was there, the same hurt in his eyes, that she'd seen in her mirror the last few days.

"What are we doing, Jax?" She sounded as resigned and broken as she felt.

His hands grabbed hers and held them tight, and he held her gaze with a ferocity that she didn't dare look away from. "Bria. I went to the airport." His words were like a knife but she refused to flinch and let him continue. "I was going to leave and take the job in California." Somehow he knew that she knew about the job but he didn't ask how. She nodded, because hadn't she thought deep down he was going to take the job? "But I couldn't get out of the truck. Something stopped me and yes, it was the food critic." Then she did flinch. He'd come back for the critic. How could he not? "But that wasn't everything. Bria, look at me." She did, despite the gaping hole he'd left in her heart. "I know I'm a thickheaded idiot. I know I'm an idiot and I know I made mistakes. Hell, I've made a lot of them. But the food critic wasn't the only reason I came back here. I came back because this is my home. Or at least it's where I want to make my home. And I knew there was a chance you'd be gone and I'm not going to lie, knowing that hurt. More than I care to admit."

She listened. There was so much she wanted to say and to ask, but she sat there and absorbed his words because it was the best thing she could do.

"If you weren't here, I was prepared to repair my life here and then come find you. Hunt you down and make you believe that this," he waved his hand, "and us…that we're worth fighting for. And we are, Bria."

She shook her head, mostly because she didn't know what else to do.

"Yes. We are."

She wanted to believe him. She wanted to take everything he said as the gospel truth. God, did she want to. But there was still so much they hadn't discussed. So much they just couldn't ignore. "But you…" She couldn't ignore it. She wanted to. But she knew she wouldn't be able to live with herself, let alone have a hope at any kind of relationship or future with him, if she didn't. "You just walked away from me, Jax," she finished. She forced herself to keep looking at him.

"I did." If she'd expected him to deny it, he didn't. And for that, he earned a few bonus points with her. She didn't think she could handle it if he pretended he hadn't abandoned her and let Slade accuse her of things she hadn't done. "And I'm a huge jerk."

Bria did a second take, not expecting him to cop to it so quickly. "What? You're not—"

ELENA AITKEN

"Yes I am." A smile twitched at his lips. "I can explain why I did it, because I think I know why. But it doesn't matter anyway. All that matters is that I did it, and I know I was wrong and…I'm so sorry, Bria." He cupped her face with his hand and looked deep into her eyes with so much intensity it made her shiver. "I was scared and I panicked. It was wrong, I was a jerk, and I want you to forgive me, Bria. Please."

She opened her mouth to say something, but shut it again when he took her face in both hands and said, "No, Bria. I *need* you to forgive me. It's been a crazy few days and I've been figuring a lot of things out, but you're the one thing I can't figure out. And the one thing I need the most. I need you, Bria, and I think you need me, too."

When she closed her eyes again, it was to force back the tears that threatened because he was right: she needed him, and she had no idea just how much until he was gone. They'd had a stupid fight, a blip really in what could be something real, but she was thankful for it because without that *blip* she never would have seen what she needed to see.

"It's crazy," she said after a moment. She shook her head and tried not to laugh because it would be a panicked, crazy laugh and she knew it. "But I totally agree with you."

"You do?"

She nodded. "I do. And none of this makes sense. But it doesn't matter. Do you know that I've spent all my adult life bouncing from one place to another? One assignment to the next with no real place to call home. And before that, my childhood home could hardly be called a home. It was cold and uninviting, and I think I would have felt more comfortable there had I been one of the fine art pieces my parents collected from all over the world, and hell, they probably would have preferred that themselves." She took a breath and gathered her thoughts so she could finish what she needed to say. To her relief, Jax stayed silent and let her

184

finish. She wasn't sure she'd be able to start again if he stopped her.

"The only place I ever felt at home was with my grandma. In most ways, I'm closer to her than my parents. Okay, in all ways." She laughed a little, diffusing some of the tension. "So I guess it's not so crazy that being here at the Springs felt good. At first I thought it was because Mona was here, but then…" It was her turn to touch him. She slid her fingers down his face, over the stubble on his cheeks he obviously hadn't shaved in the last few days. She let her thumb stroke absently while she continued, "It was you. I know we haven't known each other very long and it doesn't make any sense at all, but I don't care because I've felt more at home with you in the last few weeks than I've felt in my whole life, and when you walked away from me without even hearing my side of the story, I thought I was going to crack in two, Jax."

"I know, Bria. I'm so sorry."

"No." She stopped him. "I don't need you to apologize. I'm actually glad it happened."

"You are?"

She nodded. On the surface, none of it made any sense, but the more she thought about it, the more it crystallized in her mind. "All of this, it allowed me the chance to see what I needed to see."

"And what's that?" A smile danced at his lips and sparkled in his eyes. This man made her crazy. And she loved it.

"That I'm falling for you, Jax Carver. In fact, I think I've been falling for you from the moment I met you. Even though you drive me crazy, and push every button I have, I can't seem to help it."

Jax didn't say anything right away and there was one awful moment where Bria held her breath and thought she'd made a dreadful mistake and he didn't feel the same way. But she knew in her heart she hadn't and finally when Jax jumped to his feet and pulled her up with him, she allowed herself to breathe again. She was only able to get one quick breath in before Jax's mouth was on hers, kissing her with an intensity that left no more room for doubt. And then she kissed him back, answered his passion with her own.

"Well, you know what, Bria Sheridan?" He pulled back just enough to speak, his words puffs of air on her lips. "I love pushing those buttons and I don't intend to stop anytime soon. Especially if it means you'll do that thing with your—"

"Jax!"

She blushed, which was definitely his intent, and there was nothing left to do but kiss him again, hard. She wrapped her arms around his neck and hung on, because she was finally home.

Epilogue

NINE MONTHS LATER...

THE WIND HOWLED OUTSIDE the Grizzly Paw pub and Bria snuggled a little closer to Jax. Not that she needed a reason to get close. She'd happily snuggle with him no matter what the weather.

The last few months had been busy to say the least, but it was the best kind of busy because for the first time in longer than she could remember—she was truly happy.

She looked around the pub, and the people inside. On such a cold, blustery day—especially in off season—there probably wouldn't be many customers, not even for Archer's famous chilli. It was good, but it wasn't as good as the food Jax cooked for her.

Bria looked up at her boyfriend and couldn't help but smile.

"I don't know what put that smile on your face," Jax said. "But I like it." He kissed her softly and she melted into him a little bit more.

"I thought we were talking details," Malcolm Stone's voice interrupted them. "Save the kisses for later. This is business."

Jax reluctantly pulled away from her and laughed. "Okay, okay."

Bria sat back and listened to the details of the informal meeting Malcom was running. He was only weeks away from reopening the ski hill, and it was all hands on deck.

"Jax," Malcolm was saying. "You have the food under control? I just want appetizers, nothing too fancy. Easy to eat standing up and mingling. But nice. Like, really nice, but—"

"I got it." Jax laughed. "This is what I do, man. I can figure this out. Trust me, okay?"

Malcolm nodded, but as talented as Jax was, he didn't look convinced. Bria didn't know Malcom well. Not yet. But he seemed like the kind of man who needed to be in control of every detail. It was probably what had made him so successful in business.

But he didn't need to be worried about the food. If anyone could be trusted with that, it was Jax. Ever since the renowned food critic Augustus Bernstein had made a visit to the Springs and reviewed Jax's food and gave it the coveted five golden stars, her sexy chef was on top of his game. He was in demand everywhere. Not that he'd gone anywhere. No, together, he and Bria had decided to make Cedar Springs their home permanently.

A decision she was more than okay with. She was still finding her feet in Cedar Springs and making friends. It was going to take a bit of time after her lapse in judgement with Beth and Slade's photos. But it would come. Bria looked around the table and the room at the people she was getting to know a little bit more everyday and her eyes landed on Kylie Wilson and she smiled. Bria didn't know the other woman very well yet. But what little she did know, she liked. Maybe they'd become friends?

KYLIE RETURNED the smile Bria Sheridan gave her. She'd been a hard one to get to know at first. The woman was definitely guarded, and some said a little prickly, but there was a really nice person under that shell, and even though Kylie was still trying to get to know her, she could see it was there. Just looking at her at the table, she was different than the other women.

She held herself a little straighter, keeping a constant contact with Jax, but not in an overt way. It was subtle, but it was there. As were the little glances they kept exchanging when they thought no one was looking. They were a cute couple. Kylie smiled, and quickly tried to hide it behind her glass. It was nice that they'd decided to stay in town after finally figuring out that they really liked each other. People could be so stubborn with their own feelings sometimes.

Like she was one to talk. Kylie could have laughed at herself, and she would have too, if she wasn't sitting in what was supposed to be a meeting about the launch of Stone Summit. She'd denied her own feelings for Malcolm for so long, almost ruining everything when she'd dated his twin brother instead of him. It had taken a secret invitation to the exclusive island of Eden for Kylie to realize it was and had always been Malcolm she'd been in love with. If she'd learned anything, it was that love was not only sometimes blind, but it put a mask over your eyes and spun you around until you were so dizzy that you couldn't see straight. It was crazy making.

A gust of wind outside made the windows rattle, and Kylie instinctively drifted away from the table to the window. She gazed outside at the blizzard that had taken over main street.

It seemed so long ago that she'd been on her secret tropical island where she'd finally met the love of her life. Well, not exactly *met* for the first time. She'd known Malcolm Stone for years, but it had taken a secret invitation to an exotic island for her to realize it. What she wouldn't give to be on that island again, right now. Away from the snow and cold, and real life full of stress and busyness, she mentally added. Things had definitely better when they'd been living the fairytale. She shook her head. But fairytales didn't last forever.

Kylie left the view of the wild winter weather and went back to the table of her friends, the only ones who'd been brave enough—or stupid enough—to brave the weather. She needed to stop thinking about the island and trying to get back there for a holiday. It wasn't going to happen. There would be no more tropical holidays with Malcolm, at least not while he was preparing to re-open the ski hill just up the mountain from town. Which is why everyone was gathered today.

"Anyone need anything else to drink?"

Everyone shook their heads and gestured to the half-full jugs of beer still on the table. "Sit and join us, Kylie," Rhys Anderson said. "No more beer for these guys, or they'll all be sleeping here." It wasn't true, they'd hardly had any, but everyone laughed anyway. Rhys was the only one not drinking because he was on duty, but with the weather, it must have been a slow night, because he seemed quite happy to sit in the Paw with his girlfriend, Kari Fox, cuddled in close as if he could protect her from the cold outside.

"Okay, let's go over the final details one more time." Malcolm sat at the head of the table, running the informal meeting, and Kylie focused on her man. He looked good with his denim shirt open a few buttons and she would've been happy to take care of the rest of the buttons for him, but he was in full planning mode for the grand opening of Stone Summit. The old ski hill had been his project for longer than anyone really knew and it was finally ready to open. They were planning a New Year's Eve party to officially open the doors and no one was more excited than Malcolm. Clearly, Kylie's needs were going to have to wait. Just the way they always did lately.

She tried again to focus on the meeting that was going on. She'd been trying without much success for the last hour, but she felt restless. She pushed up from the table again and went to the bar. Technically she was still working at the moment, and even though there wasn't anyone else there, it gave her an excuse to get away.

Kylie picked up already pristine glasses and polished them further. It was mind-numbing work. A job that she normally tried to avoid, but it gave her something to focus on besides the increasing feeling of worry that kept niggling at her. She couldn't put her finger on it, but when it came to Stone Summit, and Malcolm, something bothered her. She let her gaze drift over the room to find her handsome man, who was totally in his element. He'd been working so hard that there were some days Kylie didn't even see him.

At first, after they left the island to return to Cedar Springs, things had been perfect, better than perfect. But it didn't take long for the shine to wear off and for Malcolm to start working every spare moment. And it was fine: he was an important businessman, the ski hill was a big deal, and she was just a waitress. How could she possibly understand?

"Okay, spill. What's going on?"

Sam came up behind Kylie, surprising her into almost dropping the glass. She covered her shock and smoothly finished with the glass before she turned around.

"What do you mean? Nothing's going on." She pasted a sweet smile on her face, but it was clear Sam wasn't fooled.

"Right." She slid onto a bar stool across from Kylie and leaned forward. "He's working a lot, isn't he?"

Kylie blinked hard and for a moment she considered denying it, but anybody could see how hard Malcolm worked and it wouldn't take a detective to figure out that it bothered her. She nodded and lowered her gaze.

"I totally get it." Sam let out a long sigh and propped her head up on her hand. "Grab that bottle of cabernet," Sam said. "And two glasses."

Kylie did as instructed. If anyone understood how Kylie might be feeling, it was probably Samantha Burke. She'd dated Trent Harrison, co-owner of the Springs, for about eighteen months now, and he was also a workaholic. Kylie had seen it on her friend's face lately: she was feeling the same thing. Kylie handed her friend a glass and they clinked them together.

"To busy boyfriends." But even as she said it, she knew it was more than that. Something else had been eating at her when it came to Malcolm. They'd always been friends, and he knew her better than anyone, but lately besides being too busy for her, she also felt as though she wasn't good enough for him. After all, she was only a waitress at a bar while he was opening what would no doubt be a successful ski resort. Maybe he realized he could do better.

She shook her head and tried to push the thought away. Years ago, when she'd dated his twin brother, Marcus, even though they'd had a messy relationship full of all kinds of problems, there'd been an equality. He was a snowboarder and she was a waitress. They were both on the same level. Of course he'd gone pro since then, but still...

"Whoa, slow down," Samantha said with a laugh. "You must really be worked up about something."

Kylie looked and found her glass almost empty. "Oops." She set her glass down and pushed it away. "Sorry, Sam. I know I'm working."

"I'm not worried about it. Hell, I totally get it. It's kind of hard to watch your friends have babies and get engaged like Slade and Beth, when your relationship seems to have stalled out."

That's not at all what Kylie had been thinking, and it surprised her a little that Sam was. But then again, maybe it shouldn't have. "But you are. Obviously."

"I am." Sam sighed. "Sometimes I wonder if we're ever going to get to that stage in our relationship, you know?"

Kylie nodded, even though her problem was definitely not worrying about moving on to the next stage, but wondering whether she should stay in the one she was currently in. As much as she tried not to, lately she couldn't help but wonder whether it might not be better to take a break with Malcolm.

"That's awesome!' Someone yelled from across the room, cutting her thoughts off.

Sam spun around in her stool. "What is?"

"Marcus has agreed to come for the grand opening." Rhys beamed like a little kid. Years ago, Rhys and Marcus had been snowboarding buddies, back before the hill had shut down and Marcus split to go professional. And break Kylie's heart.

Kylie swallowed hard at the mention of his name. She hated herself for it, but a million feelings rushed through her and when she finally moved her gaze around the table to look at Malcolm, she knew he'd noticed. His mouth was pressed into a thin line, his eyes dark and unreadable from the distance. But Kylie didn't need to be close to know what he was thinking. Because she was thinking it too. The last time she'd seen his twin—she'd been in love with him.

Does Kylie still have feelings for Marcus? Is Malcolm too consumed by work to be the man she needs? And what is *really* bothering Kylie? Find out next in Summit of Desire.

But first! Christmas is right around the corner in

Cedar Springs. With everyone else's relationship moving forward, will Trent and Samantha finally take the next step? Find out in She's Making A List, a special holiday novella!

You can read exclusive excerpts of both books next
——>

I appreciate you helping me spread the word about the books you love! Reviews help readers discover their next favorite read! Please leave a review on your favorite book retailer!

Don't forget to join my mailing list where you'll be the first to hear about new stories, sales and promotions and giveaways!
You can join me here —>
https://elenaaitken.com/newsletter/

She's Making A List

Please enjoy an excerpt from the next novella in the Springs Series

DESPITE THE SUN high in the sky, it was cold. More than cold, it was cover every inch of exposed skin so it doesn't instantly turn white and freeze cold. And for Samantha Burke, the bitter cold was the one thing she hated about living in the mountains. Unfortunately for her, the temperatures had been unseasonably low in the last week leading up to the Christmas festivities of Cedar Springs, festivities she normally loved both to help plan and participate in. But unless it warmed up a little, and soon, she'd be hard pressed to get excited about skating on the lake or joining in the town's Light Up celebrations.

With a sigh, she looked away from the frosty view outside the window, poured herself another coffee from the carafe on the counter and went to rejoin her friends in the living room. Carmen Kincaid, one of her best friends, had begged the ladies to come up to the apartment she shared with her boyfriend Dylan Harrison and their new son, Hunter. It was a nice place. More than nice: as one of the co-owners of the Springs resort, Dylan had a gorgeous apartment built for himself, complete with floor-to-ceiling windows that afforded brilliant views of the Rockies outside.

It was an exact duplicate of the apartment Sam shared with Dylan's brother, Trent. An apartment she'd moved into over a year ago. A move she'd felt would lead to other, more permanent moves in their relationship.

"Hey, Sam. You have to see these pictures Bria took of Hunter. They're amazing."

She shook herself out of the fog she seemed to find herself in more and more lately, and focused on Carmen, who sat on the floor, her legs outstretched in front of her, a pile of pictures scattered between them.

"Of course they are." Sam took a photo from the pile. "Hunter's way too adorable for them to be anything but amazing."

"And Bria's pretty fantastic, too," Carmen said.

Bria blushed, the way she usually did when someone complimented her work. Which was all the time, because she was an extremely talented photographer. She was also a really nice person, and even though it had taken a bit to get past the walls she put up, Sam was glad they had and now she could count both her and her boyfriend, Jax Carver, as good friends.

"Really, it's not hard to take pictures of this little guy. He's perfect." Bria didn't even look at the other women as she spoke, she was so focused on Hunter. They'd always had a special relationship. Bria had inadvertently helped Carmen with her labor, and no one was as surprised as Bria by how much she enjoyed spending time with the baby. No doubt, Jax and Bria would be the next to get pregnant.

The thought filled Sam with unexpected and totally inappropriate jealousy. Why shouldn't they have a baby? Sure, they could and some would say, should, get married first, but Carmen and Dylan hadn't. And they seemed perfectly happy in their family situation.

That's because they have a family situation, Sam thought. All she had was a live-in boyfriend. And of course she loved Trent. More than anything. But their relationship wasn't moving forward, and more and more Sam couldn't help think that it was because they'd rushed into things too soon. Maybe they weren't meant to be together forever and get married and have babies. Maybe that's not what Trent wanted. After all, they'd gotten serious quickly, and shortly after, she'd moved in to his apartment and out of her little house down in town that was now occupied by their friends Rhys and Kari.

And they'd probably be the next to get engaged.

Sam tossed the picture down on the pile and walked over to the window, avoiding the questioning gazes from all the women. She didn't want to have to admit she was burning up with jealousy for all of them. Especially Beth, her best friend, who couldn't join them for coffee because she was with her rock star fiancé Slade Black, while he finished up the last leg of his tour before the holidays. It was all too much.

"Sam?" Kari's quiet voice floated across the room. "You okay?"

She nodded, but didn't turn around. She knew it would all sound ridiculous if she tried to say anything and she didn't want any of her friends to feel bad about their own happiness. No. That was the last thing she wanted. Of course she was happy for them all. They deserved it. But so did she.

"Sam?" It was Bria's voice this time. "I'm sorry if my pictures...I mean, I could take pictures of you and Trent, too. Lots of people are doing that for Christmas this year."

She almost laughed at the absurdity of it all. Not that a photo shoot with Trent would be absurd; it might actually be fun. No, it was the idea that she was acting like a pouty child when she should be enjoying an afternoon with her friends. They didn't get the chance to spend time together much anymore and she was wasting it by feeling sorry for herself.

Sam shook her head and turned away from the window. "Thank you, Bria. That would be awesome. I'd love to have you take some pictures of us. But I know how busy you are and there's really no reason to do them."

"What do you mean, no reason?" Carmen chimed in. "How about celebrating your love? That's a good reason."

Sam snickered. "You do realize how Disney that just sounded, right?"

"She has a point." Kari agreed with Carmen, but Sam could see the woman try to hide her laughter. "It would be nice to do the pictures. Have you guys ever done any?"

"Have you?"

"We've never had a reason to."

"Exactly." Having made her point, Sam helped herself to a cookie and sat on the floor opposite Bria and the baby. "Maybe if we had a baby or were recently engaged or…" She drifted off as Hunter crawled over to her. He really was a cute little guy, and the happiest baby she'd ever seen. Sam broke off a bit of the cookie and fed it to him before Carmen could object.

She was so taken with the baby, she didn't notice right away that her friends had stopped talking. It took her a minute, but finally Sam looked up to see them all staring at her. "Stop looking at me," she snapped. "I told you, nothing's wrong. And I don't need any pictures of Trent and me, either."

"If you say so," Kari said slowly.

"I do." She gave them all a stern look before she pasted a smile on her face. "Now tell me what this little guy wants for Christmas."

Her friends dissolved in happy chatter about Hunter's first Christmas. As soon as it was polite enough to do so, Sam excused herself and let herself into her empty apartment across the hall.

Of course it was empty. Trent would be working. It's what he did. And she couldn't blame him. Not really. He'd worked really hard to get the Springs up and running, and his hard work had a lot to do with how successful the hotel was. They were always booked up and now with the new ski resort, Stone Summit, opening just up the mountain, the notoriously slower winter months were set to look just as successful.

So why then was it too much for her to expect Trent to slow down and focus on their relationship a little? Every time she mentioned that they take a holiday, he had a reason it wasn't a good time. If she wasn't such a strong, self-assured woman, she might have been worried about things between them long before now.

She pulled the afghan off the back of the couch and wrapped herself in it as she stared out at the snow coming down harder now. For a while they'd both been workaholics, doing their best to make their individual businesses successful, and that had been okay, for a time.

But people change. Things change. Heck, she'd changed.

And maybe now she wanted more.

Read the rest of She's Making A List NOW!

Summit of Desire

Please enjoy an excerpt from the next in the Springs Series

AS SHE RODE up the chairlift, Kylie Wilson took a minute to take in the view. In front of her, dozens of ski runs snaked through the pine trees and a smattering of people carved their way down the slopes in perfect S formations. With a clear blue sky overhead, they couldn't have asked for a more perfect day for skiing. Especially considering it was the official opening week of Stone Summit, her boyfriend, Malcolm Stones's, ski resort. He'd been working tirelessly for months to make the re-opening of the hill a success, but the one thing they hadn't been able to control was the weather. Fortunately, Mother Nature had been very cooperative and had provided an abundance of white fluffy snow on the ski hill that was just up from the town of Cedar Springs.

"I can't believe it's finally happening, and we'll be officially open after tonight."

Kylie turned to look at Malcolm next to her on the chair-lift. Even in his ski jacket and helmet, with goggles covering half his face, he was incredibly handsome. She smiled and leaned over to kiss him.

"It's great," she said. "And it looks like everyone's having fun."

It was true. The occasional strains of laughter floated up from the runs below to reach them on the chairlift. The town had been looking forward to the re-opening of the hill because for the people who lived in a mountain town, there was nothing more fun than spending weekends on the slopes. It had been sorely missed. To get everyone even more excited, in the week since Christmas, they'd had a "soft opening" where the townspeople of Cedar Springs had exclusive access to the ski hill. It had actually been Kylie's idea. She'd suggested that in order to be successful, they'd need to have everyone in town on board, and the best way to do that was to make them a part of the experience.

So far, it had worked perfectly.

"Are you having a good time?"

Kylie nodded but glanced away so he couldn't see her face. "I am." She wanted to add that she was having fun now that they were on the chairlift, far away from all the chaos that was taking place in the offices down below. Sitting on the chairlift with Malcolm was the first time she'd been alone with her boyfriend in weeks; except for a few stolen moments on Christmas Day, he'd been working nonstop and sure, she understood that opening an entire ski hill took work, but still. She missed him. A lot.

"I'm glad we're doing this," Kylie added, referring to the fact that they were going to take their opening day ski together. And it almost hadn't happened, as Malcolm came up with a million reasons why he couldn't get away and if she hadn't insisted, there was no doubt in her mind he'd still be in his office, working away on one thing or another. But the ski had been his idea. After all, they'd originally met at that very same ski hill many years before.

Of course, things had turned out differently back then. Kylie had ended up dating Malcolm's twin brother, Marcus, and it wasn't until a year ago when Malcolm surprised her with a secretive invitation to an exclusive tropical island that he declared his love for her, and Kylie realized it had always been Malcolm in her heart.

It was the type of happy-ever-after ending fairytales were made of, which is why everything should have been perfect between them. Should have. Kylie's smile dimmed as she thought about all the times over the last few months that she'd questioned herself and even more troubling, when she'd questioned their relationship. But she wasn't going to think about that now. Not when she was finally spending that time with Malcolm and they were together and happy. No. She shook her head hard. There was no time for those doubts now.

"I'm glad, too." Malcolm put his gloved hand over hers and squeezed. "Are you ready?"

She nodded and he lifted the safety bar as their chair approached the top of the hill and the end of the lift. Easily they each skied off and onto the ridge under the Stone Summit trail marker sign.

"Let me take your picture." Kylie sidestepped on her skis so she was in position and pulled her cellphone out of her pocket. She ignored all the text messages that had popped up on her screen. No doubt there were a ton of questions about the grand opening, New Year's Eve party that night, but they could wait for a few minutes. "Smile."

Malcolm was posed next to the sign that bore his name. She pushed the button to capture the picture. "Perfect."

"Kylie, get in here and take one with me."

"No." She shook her head. "This is your day, Malcolm. Your hill." She skied over to him.

"You're being ridiculous." He grabbed her and awkwardly pulled her toward him as much as he could with them both wearing skis. "Come on. You don't even want to take a selfie?"

She laughed, because Malcolm hated selfies and always made fun of her for taking them. He thought they were self-indulgent and silly. "Really? You want a selfie?"

"No." He took the phone from her and held it out in front of them. "But I want a picture with my girl. So come on."

She couldn't help herself; she giggled and tucked her head in next to his so he could take the shot. When he had finished, he handed back the phone and tugged his gloves back on.

"Are you ready for this?"

He looked so handsome in his ski jacket and pants. An athlete, in his element. In that moment, with both of them together, laughing, doing what they loved to do together, all of the building worries Kylie had been having melted away. It was perfect. "Let's do it."

Malcolm snapped his goggles into place. "Good, because I should get back. My phone is blowing up in my pocket." He turned and pushed off with his poles to head down the slope. And just like that, Kylie's good mood evaporated.

You're being ridiculous, she told herself. *He's just busy with this right now; it'll calm down again. Things will be back to normal again soon.* But even as she told herself that, she knew it wasn't true. Because Malcolm Stone was the type of man who was important. He made decisions, ran businesses, and created his own success. Kylie Wilson was the type of woman who still didn't know what she wanted to do with her life, and even if she did, she was too scared to do it. For God's sake, she was twenty-five and still waitressing in the Grizzly Paw pub. A successful businessman and a waitress. It wasn't the first time she'd struggled with the paradox of their relationship.

"Kylie," Malcolm called to her from a little way down the run. "Are you coming?"

No time to worry about it now anyway. She tugged her goggles on and with a strong push, skied down the hill, catching up to him in no time. If there was one thing they were equal at, it was skiing skills. And even if it wasn't much—it was something.

TAKING time out to ski with Kylie had set him back, too far back. There was way too much to do before the party that would officially signify the re-opening of Stone Summit. Malcolm had been working too hard for too long to not see the grand opening through to a final and excellent completion. It was true that the runs had been open for the last week, but it would be official after tonight, and he needed everyone, especially the competing hills in nearby towns, to know that this time Stone Summit was around for the long haul.

They left their skis propped up outside the offices, which were housed in a log building next to the main ski lodge where the cafeteria and lounge were. There were some days that Malcolm wished he would have put his offices in the lounge. It would have been easier to handle the stress if he had closer proximity to a beer now and then, but it was probably for the best that they were in a separate building.

Kylie came in with him. She pulled her helmet off and shook her dark hair out so it fell over her shoulders. God, but she was beautiful, and with her cheeks pink from the cold air outside, she looked even more perfect. His little ski bunny. Spontaneously, he pulled her into his arms and kissed her.

"Thank you," he said when he pulled away.

She laughed a little and blushed. "For what? A kiss? You know I can handle that."

"No. But that was nice, too." He brushed a strand of hair

off her forehead. "For going skiing with me. The weather was perfect and the snow, and—"

"It was just nice spending time with you." She stared straight into his eyes, challenging him. "You've been so busy lately, I feel like I haven't seen you in ages."

"I know." Guilt flashed through him, but also a flicker of annoyance. Of course he'd been busy; he was trying to open a major ski resort, practically single-handedly. Did she not get that? If he was a little busier than normal, that was to be expected. Malcolm took a breath before saying anything else. It wouldn't do anyone any good if they had an argument today. "Things will calm down again."

She nodded, but for some reason, Malcolm didn't believe that she was really okay with it.

"But for now, we're just going to have to make the best of it, okay?" He tilted her chin up so she looked straight into his eyes. "And tonight we'll ring in the New Year, okay?"

"It's going to be a crazy party, Malcolm." She shook her head gently. "There'll be people everywhere and you're going to have to—"

"Hey." She stopped and stared at him again. "It doesn't matter. Whatever craziness is going on, at the countdown, find me, okay? I want you by my side when the ball drops. I want yours to be the first face I see in the New Year and your lips to be the very first I kiss.'

She opened her mouth to object, and he laughed. "And the only lips I ever kiss," he finished. She gave him a look, but he knew she wasn't angry. "Promise me we'll ring in the New Year together."

"Of course." He kissed her again, softly until she responded to him and he deepened the kiss, enjoying a thorough exploration of her mouth. One that was long overdue.

"I'd tell you to get a room, but I don't think there are any available."

Malcolm pulled away, somewhat reluctantly, to see Sandra in the doorway to the reception area. She held a stack of files, and had a smirk on her face.

"Sorry, Sandra." Kylie slipped out of his grasp. "I was just saying goodbye."

"Sure you were." The older woman tsked, but there was laughter in her eyes, and Malcolm knew her well enough after working with her for almost the last year that she wasn't in any way offended by their display of affection. In fact, knowing Sandra, she was probably happy to see the couple spending time together. She kept telling Malcolm he was working too much, and even though he knew it was true, there wasn't any other option. Not if he wanted the resort to be successful. And he did. It had to be.

Malcolm turned to face Kylie, who'd moved back toward the door. "You're leaving? I was hoping you'd be able to help the serving staff for tonight. I'm not sure they're going to be okay with all the appetizers Jax has prepared, and I want to make sure they know what to hand out when, and how to circulate the room and—"

"I'm sure you don't need Kylie to do that." Sandra rushed into the room, dropped the folders on the desk and stood between himself and Kylie. "After all, Kylie is probably—"

"No." Kylie put her hand on Sandra's arm. Was it his imagination, or did she look upset? It had to be his imagination; just a moment ago she was melting in his arms, and...no. It was nothing. "It's fine," Kylie said. "I'm sure I could help them with a few tips or something."

"If you could, that would be great." His cellphone rang and the moment he answered it and heard the voice of Seth McBride, his general manager, on the line, all worries about Kylie evaporated. He had way more pressing issues to deal with. He turned to walk into his office so he could hear the latest report on the hill's conditions, but before he did, he put his hand over the phone and turned back to Kylie. "So you'll pop in and deal with the serving staff for me?"

She nodded, but she wasn't smiling. "I'll handle it."

"Thanks, babe. You're the best. I'll see you later, okay?"

He didn't wait for an answer, but headed to his desk to cross items off his list.

LOGICALLY, Kylie knew that whatever it was going on with Malcolm would pass. And really, she knew what it was. He was busy. Really busy. After all, he was an important businessman launching a ski resort. It was huge, really, and she was just being petty, feeling upset because he wasn't being as attentive to her as she would like. She hated herself for letting it bother her, but it did.

After leaving Stone Summit, she'd gone back to her apartment to quickly change clothes and then head over the Grizzly Paw. She'd promised Samantha she'd work her shift despite the business of the day. Sam had told her not to worry about it, considering she was supposed to be helping Malcolm with the grand opening, but there was something normalizing about working in the pub. It was who she was. Even when she pretended to be a bigger deal than she was as Malcolm's significant other, it was just that—pretending.

It only took her a few minutes to walk down the main street of Cedar Springs from her small basement suite apartment to the Grizzly Paw that sat at the end of the street, next to the frozen lake. Malcolm had tried to get her to move in with him, claiming he had a lot more room in his chalet-style house that had been built along with a few other executive homes on the ski hill, but she'd been resisting. Sure, his house was beautiful, and it made sense to live together because they spent so much free time together, but she couldn't seem to let go of her little apartment. The excuse she used was that it was easy for her to get to and from work, especially when she closed the pub. It was often too late to get in her car and drive the short distance up the mountain, especially if the weather was bad.

Six months ago, she would have made the move in a heartbeat, but things had changed between them. It was subtle at first, but the more time that went on, and the busier Malcolm got, the more Kylie realized they were from different worlds. After all, he was a successful business owner. Wealthy and powerful, and she was...a waitress in a bar. And wasn't that really the problem? She wasn't good enough for him.

The feeling weighed on her the way it had been doing more and more, and she tried to shrug it off as she walked up the steps to the Paw. Before she opened the door, she took a moment to watch the ice skaters on the lake. It was one of her favorite things to do in the winter, and besides the Christmas festival, she hadn't had a moment to get out there and skate. Maybe she could drag Malcolm out tomorrow, for the annual New Year's Day party. It was a pretty low-key event, but usually her friends would gather and go skating and drink hot chocolate and just have a little fun as a way to celebrate the new year.

But she knew it wouldn't happen. Malcolm would be way too busy to get away and she'd probably spend the day waiting for him to have time to get away. Maybe she'd just have to go on her own? With a sigh, she opened the door and stepped into the busy pub.

"Hey Kylie." Archer greeted her from the bar, where he was pulling pints. Even though it was Samantha's bar, Archer was the fixture behind the bar at the Paw or in the kitchen, cooking up his famous chili. "You know you didn't have to come in today. It's going to be slow what with the big party and all."

Kylie nodded and stripped off her heavy jacket. "I know,

but honestly? I wanted to come in." Archer gave her a questioning look but she ignored it and went into the kitchen to hang up her jacket and put her purse away. She took an extra moment before she returned to the bar, hoping Archer would forget about the question he was obviously dying to ask.

"You going to tell me why you're not up at the Summit?"

No such luck.

Kylie sighed. "I will be later."

"And now?"

"When did you get so nosy?" It wasn't like Archer to ask so many questions. That was Sam's job. Archer usually kept his head down and made silent observations, but he rarely shared them. Not unless he thought it was really important.

"Not nosy," he said with a shrug. "Just wondering."

Kylie ignored him and tied her apron around her waist. She grabbed a tray ready to go take an order, but stopped when she realized there was only one table and Archer was setting those beers on a tray.

"I told you it would be slow today." He grinned and went to deliver the drinks.

It was slow, and she knew it would be. Everyone in town was getting ready for the party up at the Summit later. Even Cynthia Giles, her best friend, who ran the general store, had closed down early to get ready. She'd tried to convince Kylie to take off with her and get her hair done at Shear Thing, but Kylie just wasn't in to it. And what was worse, she felt guilty about it. She should be excited about the party; after all, it was Malcolm's big day and she loved Malcolm. She dropped her head in her hands on the bar and rubbed at her temples.

She was being ridiculous. Just because her boyfriend was successful didn't make her a failure. She needed to remember that. And he'd never once made her feel like she wasn't good enough. That was all her.

"You okay?"

Kylie's head shot up and she ran a hand through her hair in an effort to pull herself together. "Of course. Why would you ask?"

Archer smirked. "Only because it's New Year's Eve. You should be getting ready for the biggest party of the year—one your boyfriend happens to be the guest of honor at—and you look like your dog just died."

"He did." Unwanted and totally unpredictable tears pricked at her eyelids. She hadn't cried about Ranger, her old German Shepard in months. And Archer knew it. He raised an eyebrow at her. "Okay, it's not Ranger I'm upset about."

"I know."

"It's just that…" The truth was she couldn't put a finger on why exactly she was upset. She had everything to be excited about, and nothing to cry about. Except the slight detail that the more successful Malcolm got, the more she felt she didn't deserve him.

"Hey." Archer held up his hand. "You certainly don't have to talk if you don't want to. In fact, I've had almost enough female emotional stuff in the last few weeks to last me awhile."

Kylie smiled; she knew he was referring to Samantha and Trent's recent wedding at Castle Mountain Lodge. Sam had been feeling the sting of all her friends moving on while she was being left behind, and she hadn't been shy in venting to her best friends, Archer included. Trent had surprised Sam with the ceremony and as the closest thing to family that Sam had, Archer had actually walked her down the aisle. No doubt he was relieved to have a little peace as far as Sam was concerned.

"Don't worry, Arch. I won't start crying on your shoulder or anything. Quite honestly, everything's fine."

He gave her a look that let her know that he was fully aware that she was lying, but Kylie also knew that he was smart enough to leave it alone. And for that, she was grateful.

"Well, if you want to talk…"

"Thanks."

Kylie forced a weak smile and got to work, washing tables and wrapping cutlery. There really wasn't much to do and it only took an hour for the last of the customers to leave. Everyone in town was getting ready for the party. Guilt crept in because that was exactly what Kylie should have been doing, too. Malcolm had ordered her a gorgeous dress to wear. Not that he needed to; she had plenty of things in her closet. Okay, she didn't. But she didn't need her boyfriend buying her outfits. It was becoming a trend and Kylie didn't like to feel like a kept lady. She didn't need someone to buy her things and take care of her, and more and more that was what Malcolm was doing. It irked her. More than irked her. It pissed her off.

"Time to go," Archer called from behind the bar and interrupted her thoughts, which was probably a good thing.

"It's not closing time." She grabbed up the rag she'd been using and joined him at the bar. "We're still open for another hour."

"You have noticed that you and I are the only ones here, right? It's time to go, Kylie." He took the rag out of her hand and tossed it into the sink before he squeezed her shoulder gently. "Come on. Let's go to your boyfriend's party."

She had to swallow a groan, which only made her feel guiltier.

"And smile, Kylie. It's a party. It's supposed to be fun."

READ the rest of Summit of Desire NOW!

About the Author

Elena Aitken is a USA Today Bestselling Author of more than forty romance and women's fiction novels. Living a stone's throw from the Rocky Mountains with her teenager twins, their two cats and a goofy rescue dog, Elena escapes into the mountains whenever life allows. She can often be found with her toes in the lake and a glass of wine in her hand, dreaming up her next book and working on her own happily ever after with her very own mountain man.

To learn more about Elena:
www.elenaaitken.com
elena@elenaaitken.com